THE FLIGHT

HEATHER J. FITT

BLOODHOUND
— BOOKS —

First published in 2023 by Bloodhound Books.

www.bloodhoundbooks.com

Print ISBN: 978-1-5040-8247-1

ALSO BY HEATHER J. FITT

Open Your Eyes

*For my wonderful, clever niece Lily – my little Mini-Me.
Isn't it wonderful that despite the thirty years between us, we
have writing in common?*

CHAPTER ONE

People often use the term poisons and toxins interchangeably, a bit like they do poisonous and venomous. Any sensible person though, knows something which is poisonous needs to be ingested to be harmful, and venom is injected – usually by the creature that created it.

Poisons and toxins themselves are a little more tricky. Poisons are matter which, when consumed, absorbed, or inhaled, will cause harm. Whereas a toxin is a *type* of poison, which is produced within a living cell or organism.

My personal preference is toxins. Specifically those kinds that cannot be traced, or certainly a pathologist would struggle to find unless they knew what to test for. It's all part of the fun to see if I can pull the wool over their eyes; to see if I can get away with it.

What people don't realise, and would be surprised to discover, is most of these kinds of poisons are readily available in nature, if you only know where to look for them. If you ever read Agatha Christie you would have a fountain of knowledge at your fingertips, not to mention the subsequent companion books that have been written. Where do you think my interest sparked from?

The other thing to consider is that although some poisons can be and often are lethal, they can also do some good. People far cleverer than you or I analyse the molecular structure of these plants and then use them in lower doses to treat heart failure and to help prevent complications after an operation. So you see, intention is everything.

I first read *The Mysterious Affair at Styles* when I was nine and it was then my obsession with Agatha Christie and toxins began. After I'd finished reading it, I spent all my time at the library consuming as many of her books as I could get my hands on. Not always easy, let me tell you. I then began looking up her biological murder weapons and my fascination grew. I once tried to check some of these books out, but the librarian gave me such a funny look, I stuck to reading them in situ.

People have underestimated me my whole life. They look at me and hear me speak and assume – weren't they ever taught never to judge a book by its cover? But that's okay because their misjudgement of me means they don't suspect me and as long as I hold my counsel they never will.

The first time I killed someone it was in anger, they had annoyed me. I vowed I would never do it again. Yes, I got away with it, but the remorse was all encompassing and I struggled to live with myself. The second and third times were easier, but I soon realised I could get out of control. Killing people was addictive, but I could quite easily make a mistake, and so with the exception of very recently it has been over five years since I last took a life.

I rather suspect that might change soon.

CHAPTER TWO

MELISSA

Three hours before take-off

The departure hall at Heathrow was bursting at the seams of the automatic sliding doors. There was the usual mixture of people rushing, frantic they might miss some deadline or other, and people strolling with all the time in the world. The latter always getting in the way of the former.

The vast space was filled with the constant buzz of chatter, punctuated intermittently by the voice high in the ceiling announcing flights and telling the passengers which queue they needed to be in. The lights inside were too bright and the temperature too warm after the gloom and chill of the early winter's morning. People's clothes carried the cold and a damp smell permeated the air around them. The sheer number of passengers meaning this was an all-pervading assault on the senses. Everyone desperate to get away from the horrible UK winter weather.

Melissa pushed a buggy with one hand and a giant suitcase

with the other, grateful it had four wheels instead of two. Her son Theo's bag was shoved into the gap under his seat and a rucksack strapped to her back weighed heavy on her shoulders. Melissa's old fear returned; could she really do this by herself? Travel halfway across the world with a toddler? Just carrying their luggage was proving to be difficult enough.

Melissa cut off her thoughts abruptly, reminding herself *why* she was taking her two-year-old son on a long-haul flight, to the other side of the world ten days before Christmas. She was doing it for him, everything she did was for him. Okay it was a little for her, but a happy mum made a happy child. She'd stayed with her ex, for Theo, for as long as she could, until staying was no longer the right thing to do.

She stopped to check her phone near one of the enormous automated signs that told you when your flight was due to leave and what departure gate you needed. They were in plenty of time, so much so the board hadn't even announced which queue they needed to join to check-in their bags; judging by the earlier flights they had at least forty minutes to wait.

Theo was already fractious at having been woken up so early, so hanging around waiting, *doing nothing*, and keeping Theo in his pushchair was not going to be a good option. She needed to distract him, entertain him, until it was time to go.

Melissa was trying to decide if she could be bothered with the hassle of trying to get a cup of coffee when she found herself lurching forwards, almost knocked off her feet. She grabbed at the handles of the buggy to right herself, the column supporting the announcement board stopped them from going any further.

'Hey, watch where the f–' She was trying desperately not to swear in front of Theo. Something she often failed at. 'Watch where you're going!'

'Sorry, didn't see you there,' called the man over his shoulder as he continued on his way, barely breaking stride.

Melissa felt her temper rising further and had to bite down on her tongue to keep from vocalising the stream of expletives running through her mind. How many times had she heard that? *Sorry, I didn't see you there.* Yes she was short, only 5'3", and petite, a size six, but who could really miss the mass of curly brown hair that circled her head like a halo? Melissa was sick of not being seen, not being taken seriously and ignored, just because of her size. The fact it had been happening her whole life did not mean she had learned how to handle it well.

'Mama, I hungry.'

Melissa's attention was drawn back to her son. At only two, he was still finding his words, but he knew what he wanted and when he wanted it. She seemed to spend all of her time teaching him how to make his demands in a more polite manner. She was judged harshly enough for being a young, single black woman, raising a mixed-race child, she did not want to invite further criticism because she had not taught her son good manners.

Melissa moved round to the front of the buggy so they could see each other. 'Okay, baby, but can you ask again nicely please?'

'Mama, please I have something to eat?' Theo said, his blue eyes serious.

'Good boy. Of course you can. Shall we get Mama a coffee too?'

Theo nodded furiously and the decision was made.

She manoeuvred them and their luggage over to the coffee shop and quickly realised she would have to leave her suitcase near a table, there was no way to get it and the buggy through the queuing system that had been put in place. Was anything about today going to be straightforward?

Eventually, after what felt like an interminable time of trying to juggle her coffee and the pram and the snacks she had bought, one of the baristas offered to help her back to her table. Once they were settled, she let Theo out of his buggy to stretch his legs for a while and handed him a treat. Their flight was over eight hours and he was going to be cooped up for long enough as it was. She picked up her phone for a mind-numbing scroll through social media; anything that meant she didn't dwell on the flight.

Melissa sipped at her coffee, one eye on her phone the other watching as Theo tottered around the table. His tiny trainers made his feet heavy and Melissa was reminded of the way clowns walked in their too-large shoes. Feeling calmer for being still for a few minutes, she went through her lists in her head, mentally deleting the ones she no longer needed. If she'd forgotten to pack something, it was too late. The next challenge was to drop off her suitcase and then take Theo, in the buggy, straight through security.

She was not looking forward to *that*, what with the buggy and the bags and the liquids and getting Theo to go through the scanner. She could feel her stress levels rising just thinking about it. *Stop it!* She'd deal with that problem when she came to it, no point in worrying about it now.

In her head, she moved on to Departures where she planned to find them a seat to use as base camp: somewhere near the toilets and a shop in case they wanted more snacks.

'Mama, the man.' Theo ran into her legs, one hand soft on her knee and the other pointing at some unknown person he was looking at amongst the throng of people.

Melissa looked around to see if she recognised someone. 'What man, Theo?'

'Man in the house.'

'Oh, no, that's not the same man, they just look the same.'

Theo was going through a stage of thinking anyone who looked similar was the same person. The previous week he'd thought the post lady was his nursery school teacher – presumably because they both had short grey hair.

By the time Melissa had finished her coffee, the message board had announced they were to drop their bags at Zone C. After strapping Theo back into his buggy – which he ensured everyone in the hall knew he was not happy about – and lugging the rucksack back on her shoulders, she made her way to join the queue.

At the front of the throng of people she was asked for their passports and boarding cards by the friendly airline staff member.

'Oh, shit, sorry.' Melissa winced, realising she'd sworn in front of Theo again. 'Hang on, let me just get them now.' How could she have forgotten that she needed to show their passports? She'd even made a plan to tuck them into the folds of the pushchair hood.

'Why can't people be more organised, I mean, it's not hard is it? Everyone knows you need your passport and boarding card.' The cut-glass English accent of the woman who had spoken rang clear above the din.

Melissa turned and shot daggers at the woman. She was much older and carried nothing other than a designer handbag, her hair swept into a chignon. Distracted, all Melissa could think about was how uncomfortable the hairstyle was going to be if she wanted to sleep on the plane.

Melissa's words deserted her. There were two men with the rude old bag, who both appeared to be sporting a rather large amount of luggage.

'Now, dear, she's on her own with a child. Doesn't seem to be a man about to help her,' said the smaller, balding man with a dodgy moustache.

His patronising tone made Melissa want to hiss at him, like an angry cat, as she rifled through the rucksack looking for her paperwork. She bit down on another angry, sarcastic retort.

She produced both passports and boarding cards with a flourish, grinning triumphantly at the member of staff. She was waved through with a kind smile.

'Thank goodness for that!' Again, the woman did nothing to quiet her words.

Melissa turned to aim another glare at the woman, not caring if she was seen or not, but the old cow had averted her attention to her phone.

The younger man had seen her though. 'Sorry,' he mouthed, staring at her. 'Come along, Mother, it's almost our turn.'

Melissa blushed and turned away, trying to concentrate on what she was supposed to be doing. She walked over to the machine she had been directed towards and scanned her paperwork. It asked her to place her hold luggage on the conveyor belt to be weighed. She pushed Theo out of the way and tried to lift the heavy suitcase onto the scales. Its bulkiness, combined with Melissa's small stature meant she couldn't get the necessary leverage to heave it into place.

'Mama, the man.'

Melissa ignored her son, she didn't have the time or the patience to explain how people can look the same but be different – again. Frustration started to build in her stomach and she could feel herself getting hot. She was the better part of twelve hours away from a shower and could do without any kind of BO-causing sweat.

'Can I help you with that?'

The voice caught her off guard. She had been so focused on lifting the suitcase, and ignoring rude people, that she hadn't heard him approaching. She turned and saw the young man who had been with the Wicked Witch, as Melissa had now named her.

Up close he towered over her. Melissa had to look up to see his face properly. His blue eyes twinkled as he looked at Theo and a smile grew on his lips.

'Yes, thank you, that would be helpful.' Melissa stepped out of the way, drawing his attention back to her. *Those eyes...*

He lifted the suitcase and placed it on the scales in one easy move.

'Thank you,' said Melissa, 'and sorry about...' She gestured towards Theo. 'He thinks anyone who looks similar is the same person.'

'It's fine, don't worry.' His smile was easy and she could quite happily lose herself in those eyes forever.

'Aaron? Are you finished? We need to go.'

Melissa turned towards the imperious voice and found herself face to face with the woman who she now knew was the matriarch of the family. She was unapologetically looking Melissa up and down.

Melissa stared back at her, hard, her eyes blazing. How dare she? Who the hell did she think she was? In an effort to stop herself tearing a strip off the pompous old hag, Melissa dragged her eyes away and busied herself making sure she had all of her belongings; she neither wanted nor needed a scene.

'Yes, Mother. Do you need any help with anything else?'

There was a pause and Melissa realised he was addressing the second part to her.

'No, thank you. You've been very kind.'

He smiled at her again then said to Theo, 'See you later, little guy.'

'Bye!' Theo shouted, drawing smiles from the strangers around them.

CHAPTER THREE

AARON

Aaron waved at the little boy and watched as he and his mother made their way around the check-in station and headed towards security.

'Aaron.'

His mother's abruptness was beginning to grate.

'I was only trying to be nice, Mother. You know, #BeKind?' Aaron busied himself with loading their bags onto the scales, not looking at his mum.

'Hashtag nothing. You can't save every waif you come across, you know. And what about me, do I not deserve to be a priority after everything I've done for you? What would Lydia say? Where *is* Lydia, by the way?'

Aaron turned to face his mum, who was scanning the airport crowd, and caught his dad's eye. His father raised one eyebrow and gave him a knowing look. It was a look that said, *You're about to spend eight hours on an aeroplane with this woman, do you really want to start an argument now?*

Aaron took a deep breath and tried to channel his inner zen, or whatever it was Lydia kept going on about.

'Lydia will be here with her parents shortly. They said for us to go ahead and get through security. They'll meet us in the lounge for a glass of fizz soon.'

'Really, darling? Fizz? I'm certain I taught you better than that. We must maintain standards, let's not lower ourselves to the riff-raff.'

'Sorry, Mother, champagne.' He tried to keep the sarcasm from his voice, but Vivian very nearly caught him rolling his eyes. 'The Grant-Fernsbys are just running a little behind schedule, that's all.'

'Well, I hope they turn up for the wedding on time.'

Aaron bit his tongue to stop a sarcastic retort and finished loading their suitcases. 'There. We can head through security now. Do you have any liquids in your bag?'

'You've already asked me that, dear, and yes I do. I know I've got to put them in a little plastic bag and then put them in the tray thing separately. I'm not quite going batty yet, you know.'

'And this is why I didn't bother to bring a bag. Nothing to put in the tray thing – straight through the scanner machine.' His father's Glaswegian accent was nothing more than a memory unless you listened very carefully.

'I can't believe you haven't even brought a book with you, Rex. You know how you get when you're bored,' warned Aaron's mum.

'Vivian, my darling wife, there will be movies to watch and drinks to be drunk – I doubt very much I'll get bored.'

'If you think you're–'

'Here we are.' Aaron cut his mother off before she could get up a head of steam. He handed her a clear plastic bag. 'Let's get through security and then we can get ourselves settled and relax a bit in the lounge before we have to get on the aeroplane.'

Aaron breathed a sigh of relief as they left the security gates and headed for the First Class Lounge. His mother had been under the mistaken belief that just because there was less than 100ml left in her perfume bottle, she could still carry the 150ml container. When the security guard had informed her otherwise, Vivian had demanded she be compensated for the disposed-of perfume.

'Don't you think you can get one over on me. I know as soon as we've gone you'll pull that bottle out of the bin and keep it for yourself. It's not like you'd be able to afford it otherwise.'

Aaron had turned beetroot and whispered to his mother that she was causing a scene. If there was one thing Vivian Fortescue hated, it was a scene and she quickly stopped talking.

Rex offered Vivian his arm. 'Come along, dear. Let's go straight to the lounge and get away from the rabble, shall we?'

Once in the lounge, Aaron secured a couple of tables for their party and settled his mother and father into a pair of comfortable armchairs. His offer to go and get the drinks was not so much an act born out of good manners, more one of self-preservation. He needed just a few minutes away from the constant expectations and fault-finding.

After taking as long as he possibly could, including allowing someone ahead of him in the queue, he returned to the table with a glass of champagne for Vivian and a measure of whisky for Rex. Aaron had opted instead for a bottle of beer, and determinedly ignored his mother's glare when he drank it straight from the bottle.

He loved his parents dearly, he really did, but their snobbish outdated ways drove him to distraction at times. His mother had grown up with it of course, but his father had no choice and it was forced upon him lest he embarrass his in-laws. Aaron wasn't sure which was worse: for someone to be so unkind because their position afforded it, or for someone to forget what it was like when people were unkind to them.

Rex wasn't even Aaron's father's real name. He had been christened Brian, however that had been deemed to be far too common and the nickname – given to him in honour of Rex Harrison by Vivian since she loved *Dr Doolittle* as a child – had been used ever since.

Aaron's maternal grandparents had never envisaged their daughter would marry a man from a shabby part of Glasgow. No, that had been thrust upon them when Vivian had confided in her mother she was pregnant; the wedding coming quite swiftly after that, and no one was given any choice in the matter, least of all his father.

It all sounded a little too similar to his own situation – not that Lydia was pregnant of course, they'd been far too careful for that. It was more that he felt he hadn't had a choice in the matter. He and Lydia had been a couple for several years and it felt like the whole world had been dropping hints that it was time he proposed. So he did just that.

Except now, he wasn't quite sure he should have. Did he really love Lydia? Was he just trying to keep other people happy? Did Lydia really love him? That was a question he didn't know the right answer to. He thought so, but there was a nagging doubt there that made him think she had some kind of hidden agenda. But then, that made the feeling sound too strong.

'Aaron!'

The sound of his name being shouted across the lounge cut through Aaron's preoccupations. He turned and saw his friend, and best man, Darius Johnson, making his way towards him; his bulky frame making him look too large for the surroundings.

'What is *he* doing here? More to the point, how did he get in here?' hissed Vivian.

'I paid for him, Mother. Be nice,' replied Aaron quietly. The smile never left his lips as he watched his friend winding between chairs, apologising as he inevitably bumped into people.

Aaron and Darius had met while they were at boarding school together and had been firm friends ever since, much to his mother's dismay. Darius was a typical and slightly brash American, who Vivian considered to be uncouth. Aaron also suspected, although his mother would never admit it, she had a problem with the colour of his skin too.

'Good to see you, my friend,' said Aaron as they embraced in a manly hug with plenty of back-slapping. 'No problems getting in?'

'No problems at all.' Darius lowered his voice. 'I can't tell you how much I appreciate everything you're doing, man.'

'It's my pleasure.' Aaron matched his volume before saying more loudly, 'You remember my mother and father, Vivian and Rex?'

'Of course, how could I ever forget.' Darius showcased his most charming smile.

Rex rose to his feet, his hand outstretched. 'Good to see you again, son.'

Darius shook the man's hand quickly. 'You too, Mr Fortescue, you too.'

Vivian did not rise to meet her son's friend, merely regarded him coolly. 'Darius,' she said with a small incline of her chin.

'Mrs Fortescue, radiant as ever.' Darius swept in to plant a kiss firmly on her cheek.

Aaron saw his mother's eyes widen and he knew she was desperately trying not to flinch.

He clapped a hand on Darius's back to distract his attention. 'How about a beer?'

'Sure, sounds good to me. Everything going according to plan?' Darius raised an eyebrow.

'So far, so good.'

When Aaron and Darius returned from the bar, Vivian was reading her Kindle and Rex was playing with his phone. After spending a peaceful few minutes chatting with Darius, Aaron's phone beeped, interrupting them.

Aaron fished the phone from his pocket. 'It's Lydia, apparently they're struggling to find the lounge.'

'Struggling to read those enormous signs, are they?' Darius didn't conceal his sarcasm.

Aaron rolled his eyes and glared at Darius who held up his hands defensively.

'Sorry, sorry. I promise I'll behave from now on. Do you want me to go and find them?'

'No, I'll go. If you go, she'll only get herself into a huff.' Aaron stood. 'Could you get a couple of glasses of champagne though please? And a whisky and ginger for Archibald?'

'Sure.'

'Don't know why he wants to ruin good whisky with that ginger nonsense,' said Rex, suddenly attentive when another drinks order was being made.

'You could refresh our glasses while you're there too, Darius.' Somehow, Aaron's mother had managed to phrase the sentence as both a request and a command.

'Of course, Vivian.' Darius almost bowed.

Aaron shared a look with his friend and then left to find his fiancée and future in-laws.

'I was about to send out a search party! Thought you might've done a runner.' Darius winked at Aaron and Aaron fired back a knowing look.

It had taken him more than twenty minutes to find Lydia and her parents, and escort them back to the First Class Lounge. Aaron was just about at breaking point already and they still had the entire flight to go, not to mention boarding and disembarkation.

He ushered Lydia and her parents, Archibald and Daphne, over to where his mother and father were sitting.

'What an absolute *nightmare*,' huffed Lydia. 'You would think the staff might actually *know* where the First Class Lounge was.'

Daphne patted her daughter's hand. 'Never mind that now, darling. We're here and we have champagne. Let's just try to relax.'

Archibald Grant-Fernsby made a kind of grunting noise at the back of his throat, which Aaron had learned was his 'agreeing' noise.

'Your mother is quite right, sweetheart. Let's just relax and enjoy the hospitality.'

'Hmph, champagne's not even cold.' Lydia was in one of her moods.

Aaron watched his fiancée as her mother tried to calm her down. It was so obvious she was spoiled, and he tried to remember what had first attracted him to her. He struggled to remember, but he was certain she hadn't always been this bad, had she?

Lydia was wearing an all-white outfit, with ridiculously high wedged sandals. Her make-up was flawless, as always, and there was not a hair out of place from where it had been twisted into a bun on the top of her head. Aaron felt uncomfortable just looking at her and it dawned on him, at some point, mid-flight, she was going to realise she had picked the wrong wardrobe and he was going to bear the brunt of her complaining.

He was going to need another beer.

CHAPTER FOUR

MELISSA

Melissa had been grateful for the help, but she had no desire to be anywhere near that woman again. Instead of going straight through security, she decided to change Theo's nappy on this side, and put some distance between them. She suspected they would end up in a lounge somewhere, probably first class, sipping champagne, so she was unlikely to see them again.

Melissa thanked whichever bright spark had come up with the idea of making the toilet cubicles bigger in airports. The baby changing one was large and bright, and it meant she had plenty of space for everything, including the buggy. Changing Theo's nappy wasn't quite the ordeal she had envisaged.

Deciding she had given that awful woman more than enough time to clear security, Melissa took a deep breath and headed that way herself. Theo's eyelids were staying closed for longer and longer each time he blinked and Melissa could see his head start to fall forward. She gently shook the buggy and told him they were about to have an adventure and he needed to wake up to see.

That seemed to do the trick and Theo was wide-eyed,

watching everything going on around him, squealing in delight, his little hands waving in the air. Melissa whizzed around the retractable queue barriers making a 'whee!' sound as she did so and was delighted to hear Theo giggling.

When she arrived at the scanner she arranged everything in the trays as instructed, pulling out her laptop and Kindle she placed them in separate trays. Next she had to remove her footwear, cursing herself for opting to wear boots. Those wearing sandals were able to keep theirs on, but it was five bloody degrees outside and there was no way she was flashing her toes in that kind of temperature.

Melissa lifted Theo. 'Come on, buddy, we need to walk through the machine.'

She set him down while she collapsed the buggy and put it on the conveyor belt. As she turned around she realised Theo had taken advantage of her distraction and shot off without her.

'Wait for Mama, Theo.' She caught up with him and picked him up with a playful roar in his ear, tickling him. 'And where do you think you're going?'

Theo giggled and squirmed in her arms as she made her way back to the metal detector and waited her turn.

'Excuse me, madam?'

'Yes?' she said distractedly, still tickling her son.

'I'm afraid your son will need to walk through on his own.'

'But he's only two,' Melissa snapped.

'I appreciate that, madam, but because he can walk, he'll need to go through by himself. He can keep his shoes on though.'

'I should hope so!' Melissa didn't really want to let Theo go, he'd already tried to escape once, but she couldn't argue, could she? The security guard had already seen Theo's runaway trick.

The second guard had a friendlier face. 'Don't worry, madam, I'll make sure he doesn't run off. What's his name?'

'It's Theo, and thank you.'

Melissa set Theo down on his feet and explained he needed to walk towards the nice man calling his name. Theo looked at her for a second and then realised he was free! He took off anew, his little clown shoes accentuating his waddle.

The security guard on the other side swept him up in the same way as Melissa had. By the time Theo realised he didn't know the man and started to look worried, Melissa was through and reaching out for him.

She made her way to the conveyor belt to collect her belongings, the floor cold through her socks. As she approached the end of the belt, she could see her things beginning to come through. All at once, the size of the task ahead hit her in the chest and made her gasp. Panicking, she realised she still needed to collect all of their belongings, assemble the buggy and strap Theo into it without him making another break for freedom.

She took a deep breath.

One thing at a time.

The buggy was one of those you could unfold with one hand and a foot, so she grabbed that first and left everything else on the conveyor belt. Once Theo was strapped in, she could breathe again and take her time getting everything together.

That was a great plan, right up until Theo decided he didn't want to sit in his pram after his taste of liberty and began to cry, although 'ear-piercing wail' may have been a more accurate description of the sound coming out of his tiny mouth.

Melissa had no choice but to carry the rest of her things over to a table and ignore Theo's sobs. She spoke to her son softly and reassured him he wouldn't be there for long, all the while putting things back in their rightful place and her boots on.

She could feel eyes on her from all over the security hall, like daggers stabbing into her skin. Her cheeks flushed. What did these people expect? Did they think she liked it when her son cried? Did they not realise if she knew precisely how to get him to stop crying, she would have already done whatever it was?

Finally everything was where it belonged and mercifully Theo's wails were just a soft whimper. She hefted the rucksack onto her back and wheeled Theo towards the lift. The rubbing of the wheels joined the hubbub of the crowds, the noise loud in her ears.

Once in the main part of the departure lounge, she bought herself a coffee and lots of snacks for both of them. She then pushed Theo to a quiet area where there was plenty of space for them to spread out and Theo could come out of the pushchair.

Ninety minutes, two tantrums and two chocolate-button bribes later, Melissa heard the call for her flight.

'It's time to get on the aeroplane, Theo. Won't that be exciting?'

'Plane?'

'Yep, it's time for us to go. You want to get in your pushchair?'

'Yeah!'

Melissa watched in amazement as Theo climbed into the buggy by himself and tried to do up the straps. *Note for future reference: aeroplane bribes work!*

At the gate, Melissa made her way to the desk and identified herself to the flight attendant as she had previously been instructed.

'Hi, I'm Melissa Young. I was told I might be able to get help and board early?'

'Hi, Melissa, I'm Amanda. That's no problem at all, just take a seat over there and I'll let you know when we're ready for you.

We'll get you on board first and then you can get the wee one settled.'

Melissa did as she was instructed and took the seat nearest the desk. Through the enormous glass windows, she could see the gloomy winter daylight, and occupied Theo by pointing out the aeroplanes they could see taking off from the runway.

'Look, Mama!'

The little boy's excitement drew smiles from those around her, and she smiled back.

'He's adorable.' The woman who spoke looked like every grandmother from every family film you'd ever seen.

'Thank you. Although I'm not sure you'll be saying that when he's throwing a temper tantrum halfway through the flight.'

'Ah, don't worry. I'm sure he'll be fine.'

Before Melissa knew it, Amanda was standing before her and telling her it was time for them to embark.

'When you get to the aeroplane door, they'll take the buggy from you there and someone will help you get settled.'

'That's great, thank you.'

'Excuse me! *Excuse* me!'

The voice sounded familiar to Melissa and when she turned, she closed her eyes in disbelief.

'Yes, madam? Can I help you?'

'Yes, I'd like to know why this... *young lady* is boarding before us? We have priority boarding and we paid for it.' She smirked, the insinuation clear.

'Of course, madam, and you and your party will be the very next people to board. However, this lady needs assisted boarding and that takes precedence.'

'Why on earth should she need assisted boarding? The last time I checked being a single mother did not make you disabled.' She managed to make the words 'single mother' sound disgusting. The woman turned her attention to Melissa. 'Young lady, if you cannot cope with a child by yourself, perhaps you should not be going on holiday? Or perhaps you should not have found yourself to be in such a position without a husband.' Bitterness and distaste oozed from every part of her body language.

Melissa was close to losing it completely. From the moment she had decided to leave, the planning, packing, getting to the airport and arriving at that moment had been one of the most stressful periods in her life. She had planned and organised to the very best of her ability and yet she still hadn't realised how hard it was going to be. When she'd arrived at her departure gate she had been relieved she was finally going to get a little help. And then this... *woman* had come along and been rude to her – again.

Tears filled Melissa's eyes, whether of hurt or anger, she did not care. She wiped them away furiously, embarrassed that so many people were seeing her cry. A broken promise to herself of no more crying only added to her simmering anger.

'And now she turns on the waterworks.' Cruella de Vil threw her hands up in exasperation.

'How dare you!' Melissa's voice was low and calm, even as she spoke through the tears. 'You don't know me. You don't know anything about me, but you stand there and judge me?'

'I think I can safely say I'm quite glad I don't know you and nor would I ever want to.'

Melissa stared at her, wild-eyed. She looked at the people around her and saw, what must have been, her own expression mirrored back.

'Madam,' said Amanda quite forcefully, 'please take a seat and we will be with you shortly.'

The older woman opened her mouth to say something else, but she was quickly interrupted.

'Mother? What's going on?'

'Your mother was enquiring as to why we were not being boarded first,' said the man's father.

'*Your mother* was being downright rude, actually.' Melissa made no mistake with her eye contact. Her hands gripping the pushchair handles as she tried to restrain her fury.

'Sir, would you mind taking your mother to a seat and we'll have you all on board as soon as possible.'

'Of course.' The younger man turned to Melissa. 'I am so sorry if my mother has upset you, she sometimes speaks without thinking.' His expression was full of apology.

The old woman's face turned red and her eyes sparked, her lips pressed together. She stalked off muttering something about lodging a complaint with the management.

'I appreciate the apology.' Melissa offered a ghost of a smile, holding his look for a moment before turning to give the flight attendant their boarding passes and passports.

'Are you okay?' asked Amanda in a quiet voice.

Melissa didn't trust herself to speak without breaking down, so she just nodded, keeping her eyes on the desk in front of her.

Once through the gate and out of the sight of staring eyes, Melissa took a moment to compose herself. She pulled a tissue from her pocket, wiped her eyes and blew her nose. They were finally getting away and she'd be damned if she was going to let an ignorant, rude old lady spoil their enjoyment. She'd sworn she wouldn't ever let anyone talk down to her again, and she felt a tiny flicker of pride at having stood up for herself.

'Okay, Mama?'

She looked down to see Theo staring up at her with sad little eyes. 'Mama's fine,' she said with a big grin. 'Shall we get on the aeroplane now?'

'Yeah!'

'Let's go!' Melissa only wished she was so easily distracted.

CHAPTER FIVE

CHARLEY

Thirty minutes before take-off

'Thanks for the heads-up, Amanda.' Charley replaced the intercom phone in its cradle and peered up the ramp, waiting for a young woman and her toddler to make their way down from the departure gate.

Her colleague called to let her know the woman was upset after another passenger had shouted at her for pushing in. Apparently the young woman had done no such thing, merely responded to the call for her to come forward. She and her little boy were being boarded first so they could get settled before the long flight and an older, posh lady – Amanda's words – had taken great offence to the fact she was not being given priority.

Charley had already attended the pre-flight briefing and she knew that although there were a few children on the flight, Theo Young was the only toddler. She already had the seat belt extender ready for Miss Young to use during take-off and landing, but experience told her the little boy wouldn't want to be sat on his mother's lap for the whole flight, and likely Miss Young wouldn't want that either, so Charley had made sure there were some crayons and some paper in his seat pocket.

Charley also knew from the briefing that there was a destination wedding party coming on board which would be taking up much of first class; leaving one vacant seat. A variety of scenarios ran through her head and she just hoped they were the happy, excited kind of wedding party who booked first class seats. Amanda had told her, though, that the 'older posh lady' who had upset Melissa Young was a member of the party and that didn't bode well.

In the distance, Charley could hear the thrum of a buggy being pushed down the ramp and she fixed on a warm smile, ready to greet the young woman and put her mind at ease.

As Miss Young rounded the final corner, Charley raised her hand in a wave, but could see the young woman was still distressed.

'Hi, I'm Charley, the inflight service manager today. You must be Miss Young and is this Theo?'

'Yes.' Melissa sniffed, bending to release her son's harness.

'Shall I give you a hand? That way we can get you settled and everything stowed away before we let the rabble on.'

'Th-thank you. Sorry, I don't normally...'

'Don't you worry about that. Why don't you take Theo, and I'll sort out the buggy and then bring this bag along to your seat. Do you know where it is? On the left right behind the bulkhead at the start of the economy seating. I'll meet you there in a minute.'

A few minutes later, Charley made her way along to where Melissa and Theo were making themselves comfortable. Theo was sitting in the window seat, entertaining himself with a wooden book and Melissa was trying and struggling to get her rucksack into the overhead locker.

'Here, let me,' she said, gently taking the bag from Melissa. 'Do you need anything out of it now?'

Melissa shook her head.

'Once we're in the air, if you need it down, just press your call button and someone will come and help you. Same with Theo's bag, do you need anything out of here?'

'No. Thank you for your help. I'm sorry I'm not very chatty...'

Charley lowered her voice and leaned in towards Melissa. 'My colleague told me about that dreadful woman. I'm so sorry you had to go through that. She's sitting up in first class, so at least you won't have to put up with her in here. I can spit in her food if you want me to, or maybe slip a sleeping pill into her pre-flight champagne?' Charley said with a conspiratorial wink.

Melissa laughed and Charley saw her shoulders relax a little. 'That's very kind of you, but I wouldn't want you to get into any trouble.'

'Don't you worry about me, I've taken on worse than her and won. I need to get back up front to greet them all, so here's the seat belt extension, you'll need that for landing and take-off. Can I get you a sneaky drink before I go? Maybe a juice for Theo?'

'That would be fantastic. Any chance of a gin and tonic?'

'Say no more.' Charley gave another wink.

After delivering Melissa's drink, Charley made her way back to the front of the plane to check on her colleagues. The first class passengers were already boarded and being looked after by another member of the cabin crew.

Charley watched as her colleagues greeted the remaining passengers and instinctively began mentally assessing them. A major part of cabin crew training centred around identifying able-bodied persons, those who could help in the event of emergency, but equally as important was picking out those who might cause her or her staff a problem.

Satisfied everything was under control, Charley made her way up the brightly lit, almost glittering, staircase to the upper deck and the first class cabin. She was always amused to see people's reactions the first time they saw such a magnificent staircase on board an aeroplane. It wasn't quite so funny when they realised only first class passengers were allowed to use it though. A little luxury was always welcome, but personally, Charley thought the waterfall complete with orchid was a bit too much.

At the top of the stairs, before entering the first class cabin, Charley paused for a moment. Sometimes she could turn on her professional persona like a switch, other times she needed a minute to pull it on like a cloak. She tucked the long fringe of her chestnut hair behind one ear, lifted her chin and walked into the cabin.

Charley allowed herself a roll of her eyes, the first thing she heard was a rather pompous voice declare, 'I was only saying what everyone else was thinking.'

'Regardless, Mother, some things just shouldn't be said.'

'I agree with your mother, Aaron. What was that woman doing taking a toddler on a long-haul flight by herself? It was clear she couldn't cope, how is she going to get on when she arrives in Barbados?'

'Can we just drop it?' The younger man, Aaron, had seen Charley entering and looked rather embarrassed. 'We're on our way to our wedding, perhaps we can just relax and enjoy the hospitality these fine people have to offer.' He looked at Charley hopefully.

She decided to help him out. Amanda had said how he'd apologised to Melissa on his mother's behalf and it wasn't his fault the woman seemed to be an absolute cow.

'Good morning, everyone,' she said. 'How are we all today?'

Aaron thanked her with his eyes. 'Wonderful, thank you.'

'Why don't you settle yourselves into your seats. You are the only people making use of this cabin, so do feel free to sit wherever you choose. Can I help anyone with their hand luggage at all?'

Charley took her time making sure each of the passengers was comfortable and showed them how the gadgets in their individual pods worked: including how to fully recline their seats into a bed, if they so wished.

'Now, this is what I'm talking about!' The man Charley believed to be Aaron's father, Brian Fortescue according to her notes, was not the subtle, understated kind of rich person.

'Rex, do you really have to be so uncouth? It's not like you haven't flown first class before. Please try to show some decorum.'

Charley turned away to hide her amusement. Mrs Fortescue might be a rude, mean old lady, but she didn't discriminate.

Smoothing the smirk from her lips, Charley smiled pleasantly and turned back to face the wedding party.

'Can I get anything for anyone before I help my colleagues see to the remaining passengers?'

'I think we'd like champagne all round please,' said Mrs Fortescue before anyone else could get a word in.

'Actually, I'd like a beer instead please,' said Aaron.

A man around Aaron's age, a Darius Johnson, jumped in. 'Make that two.'

'And Archie and I will have a wee whisky. Won't we, Arch?'

Mrs Fortescue made a harrumphing noise and rolled her eyes. 'Fine, three glasses of champagne and whatever it is they have asked for.'

'Actually, could I just have a sparkling water please?' This came from the woman who could only be described as a model, sitting next to Aaron Fortescue. She swept three fingers over her bleach-blonde hair and she went back to her magazine without waiting for a reply.

'Still? Did you go to see the doctor, dear? You know it's not normal feeling under the weather for so long. Maybe we'll see if we can find you one when we get there, you wouldn't want to spoil the wedding now, would you?' said Vivian.

'Perhaps we could discuss my medical history another time.' Lydia gave Charley a pointed look.

'I'll just go and get those drinks for you now.'

As Charley walked away she heard Vivian Fortescue stage-whispering, 'Are you quite sure you're not pregnant?' Followed by Aaron hissing, 'Mother!' at the same time as Lydia said, 'Oh my God!'

CHAPTER SIX

LYDIA

Lydia could not *believe* Vivian had brought up pregnancy *again*. And this time in front of her parents, not to mention the flight attendants who were pretending not to hear. How could they *not*? It was a spacious cabin, but it wasn't *that* big.

'Vivian, I've told you time and time again, I am *not* pregnant. If I were, I would most certainly have told you if only to get you to shut up about it.'

'Well, I–'

But Lydia wasn't finished. 'Not only have you asked me yet again, but you have now worried my parents and discussed my medical history in front of perfect strangers. I will *not* keep quiet and allow you to do it any longer.'

Vivian clutched at her throat and turned to her son to defend her. 'Aaron?'

'I'm sorry, Mother, but Lydia is right. It simply isn't proper to discuss something so private in company. Come now, you must see that.'

'But I thought that's what families did? Aren't we to be a

family now? Have I misunderstood? I was merely taking an interest in my daughter-in-law's health.'

'We *are* to be a family, Mother, of course we are, but perhaps you could pick your time and place, and *company* a bit more carefully?'

Vivian tutted and prodded at the call button, even though there were at least two flight attendants within hearing distance.

Lydia leaned back in her seat and closed her eyes. The creamy leather of her first class seat felt soft and comforting, but she was finding it difficult to relax. She couldn't wait for the flight to take off so she could tune into a film on her own private screen and tune *out* of whatever drama her mother-in-law decided to get into. For someone who hated it when people argued in public, she sure seemed to start a lot of them. *One rule for one...*

Lydia hadn't felt right for a while, but there didn't seem to be any rhyme or reason to her symptoms and the doctors were struggling to find a diagnosis. She'd done multiple pregnancy tests and they were all negative. She wasn't surprised, she and Aaron were careful. A baby at this stage wouldn't be a particular issue, but she would never have heard the end of it from Vivian, who liked things to be done 'properly'.

There had been some discussion about a B12 deficiency, but Lydia wasn't convinced. She ate a well-balanced, calorie-controlled diet 95% of the time and the supplement her doctor had suggested didn't seem to be working. Or perhaps, as her GP had said, she was expecting too much too soon.

Most of the time, Lydia could cope well enough with whatever was going on, she'd learned to hide her pain and frequent trips to the bathroom. It was the most recent problem which horrified her most of all though – her hair had started to fall out. She wasn't just talking about strands in a brush either, in some cases there were great big clumps of hair missing from her scalp.

Thankfully, she was good at styling her hair and was able to hide the patches from nosey eyes. It was one of the reasons her hair was pulled into a tight bun for travelling, it was the easiest way to hide the bald spots, but she knew it would give her a headache eventually, as well as being uncomfortable for napping.

Her greatest fear was that Aaron would find out and call off the wedding. She would of course tell him afterwards, but he'd seemed a bit distant recently, like there was something on his mind and she didn't want to hand him any excuses. He knew she had been to see the doctors and a specialist and the tests were ongoing. He'd even suggested he come with her for moral support – she had declined. It was very sweet of him, but she didn't want him there, and she was fairly certain Aaron didn't actually want to be there either.

She knew he had only offered out of a sense of duty. In the same way she felt he'd only asked her to marry him – because it was *expected*. Lydia was happy with that particular part of his conscience; it was a relief when he finally proposed. She was sure though he didn't love her in the truly romantic way, but she was equally sure he didn't realise that – yet. As long as she could get him down the aisle and he said 'I do' once he was there, that was enough for her.

'Lydia?'

Aaron's voice broke into her thoughts and she opened her eyes, turning to look at him questioningly.

'Your water's here,' he said with a nod.

'Oh, thank you.'

'Are you okay? I thought maybe you'd fallen asleep.'

'I'm fine,' she said a little irritably. 'But I wish your mother would keep her nose out.'

'She cares, that's all.'

'No, she's nosey.'

Aaron winced at Lydia's words. 'We won't be spending all that much time with her once we're there.'

'Yes, just the eight or nine hours in a confined space to get through first. Excuse me, I need to go to the bathroom.'

Lydia hauled herself out of her seat, which was encased in its own little pod. Why was there no way to stand up on an aeroplane without looking like a tortoise trying to right itself?

She made her way to the toilet and locked herself inside. The toilets in first class looked like something straight out of a five-star hotel or a Michelin-starred restaurant; there were flannels and proper towels, flowers even. She had no need to use the facilities, but she needed some breathing space from her soon-to-be in-laws. Ironic that she found it easier to breathe in this small room than in her luxurious first class seat.

Lydia looked in the mirror and mentally gave herself a talking to. No matter what happened, getting to Barbados and marrying Aaron was her number one priority; her parents were counting on her and she could not, *would not*, embarrass them. Especially in front of the Fortescues.

Once she had that ring on her finger, then she could relax, start laying down the law a little more. After all, she would be the mistress of her own home. She was certain Aaron would go along with whatever she wanted, he was honourable. He also liked an easy life and was unlikely to make any waves. Once she was officially Mrs Aaron Fortescue, the possibilities were endless.

She was at the point of giving up and moving on when he had finally popped the question. Of course she said yes, she would have been mad not to. Trying to find another eligible bachelor with Aaron's wealth who she could stand to be around would have been virtually impossible.

'But are you actually *in love* with him?' This from her friend, Clarissa.

'What does that matter? I like him, he's good looking, easy to get along with and he adores me. Love doesn't last anyway – it's just a short-term thing. It's what comes after the love that's important and Aaron and I already have that. Call it companionship, if you like.'

'And it has nothing to do with him being rather wealthy?'

For a moment, Lydia had wanted to slap her friend. How dare she insult her like that. 'You're forgetting one thing – my family is rather wealthy too. I don't need a man for his money any more than you do.' Her voice was acid.

Clarissa had quickly dropped the conversation and moved on to something else. Lydia, however, could not shake it from her mind. Why would her friend assume she was marrying Aaron for his money? What had she heard?

In order to put a stop to any rumours of a similar ilk, Lydia had offered to pay for her bridesmaids' hotel and flights to Barbados. It had cost her an absolute fortune – thank God for Amex. They would be arriving in a day or two.

Clarissa had not been invited.

Lydia dampened a paper towel and blotted it across her face, careful not to remove any make-up. It had been sometime since Aaron had seen her without make-up and she wasn't about to start now – long-haul flight or no long-haul flight. Plus, she wouldn't give Vivian the satisfaction of having something else to complain about.

As she opened the door, Lydia came face to face with the flight attendant who had helped them earlier.

'Are you okay? Can I get anything for you?'

'I'm quite all right, thank you.'

'If you need any–'

'I'll be sure to let you know.'

Lydia made her way back to her seat, looking forward to cocooning herself inside her suite for one.

'Are you okay?' Aaron asked.

'I really wish everyone would stop asking me if I'm okay,' she snapped. 'I'm fine,' she said, lowering her voice. 'I just wish people would realise my private life is not for public consumption.'

Aaron reached over and patted her hand. 'Why don't you read your magazine for a bit? Or watch a film? I'm sure everything will seem much better soon.'

Inside Lydia screamed. Aaron, wonderful pleasant Aaron, always playing the peace-keeper, always trying to make people happy. For once, she would really just like to see him lose it. She wondered if he was even capable.

CHAPTER SEVEN

I have always been something of a people watcher. For some reason folk don't think it of me and it means I can get away with it all the more easily. I don't mean that they don't see me, they do, at least in the literal sense of the word. What I mean is, people think they know me, they think that what they see is what they get. They couldn't be more wrong.

Family, friends and strangers alike would be shocked if they knew about the things I noticed. An airport is a wonderful place to people-watch. They seem to feel safe there, as if everyone who is travelling somewhere is a good person. As if nothing bad can creep through the security checks, X-rays and scans. They take care over their belongings, not because they think someone might steal them, but because they don't want to be the one to cause a security alert and ruin the start of everyone's holiday, or their own.

And that is the reason why people are more relaxed – at least they are once they arrive in the departure lounge – and lower their inhibitions. Having a pint no matter what time your flight is has become something of a British tradition. Not forgetting the purchase of duty free you wouldn't even look twice at anywhere else.

All of this makes it so much easier to catch people doing things they wouldn't want their nearest and dearest to see. All you just have to do is pay attention.

Like the man I saw sneaking in and out of the disabled toilet with a woman I knew wasn't his wife. I knew that because afterwards he walked up to his spouse and kissed her full on the lips in front of everyone. So disrespectful, and that's before we even start to wonder about when they met and how they agreed to such an intimate activity so quickly.

I saw the way that ghastly woman's lip curled as she looked at her son's best friend – her son's *black* best friend. How she avoids being close to him whenever possible – always placing herself a few paces away.

Or the pickpocket I saw audaciously removing cash from a wallet before 'finding' it and handing it back to its rightful owner. A man who was so grateful he didn't even think to check the contents before he replaced it in his back pocket; the exact pocket the thief had retrieved it from in the first place.

Or the man I saw slip a pill into a woman's drink in a bar once. Never fear, dear reader, I made certain he was in no position to do her any harm.

These observations used to serve no purpose other than to amuse me, but recently that has changed. I have found myself becoming angry at the lack of basic common decency, and the urge to make a difference in the world has been strong. I have resisted to the best of my ability because there is only one way I know of to make the world we live in a better place, but it is so *final*.

Although, is that really such a bad thing?

CHAPTER EIGHT

MELISSA

Eight hours to landing

Theo had finally calmed down and was playing quite happily in his seat. Melissa was grateful to Charley for supplying crayons and paper for him to play with, and the table that pulled out from the arm rest meant he was pinned and couldn't go anywhere.

Melissa still felt wrung out – the weeks leading up to their departure had been hell on earth and although they were finally on their way, she could not relax.

Her ex-boyfriend, Ryan, had not been very accepting of the fact he was her ex-boyfriend. It had taken her far too long to realise that the way he'd treated her, the restrictions he placed on her life, were not okay. She'd lost count of the times she'd thought, or said, 'At least he doesn't hit me.'

The night she realised there was something really wrong, she was out with friends. They were all laughing uproariously at something someone had said, when Ryan appeared at their table. She hadn't seen him coming, but when she looked up and saw him, his eyes bored into hers and her stomach clenched. Every single happy thought, every ounce of humour drained from her as soon as she saw him and noticed the set of his jaw. He wasn't supposed to be there, this was *her* night, with *her* friends. Ryan was supposed to be with his mates, that was the whole reason Melissa had asked her colleague to look after Theo. Her sudden change in mood and anger towards him for turning up out of nowhere, were enough for her to realise she wasn't in a normal relationship.

When they'd arrived home that night, they'd had a blazing row; she'd screamed at him. Ryan had wanted to know why she had such a problem with him being there. They were a couple, why wouldn't she want him there? If she loved him, why did she need time apart from him? Was she seeing someone else? The whole conversation drove her crazy. There was something about the way he said it that made her think he might have a point, but she *knew* deep down this wasn't healthy.

A few days later she'd moved out and almost immediately she felt a weight had been lifted from her shoulders. She hadn't realised it at the time, but she had felt trapped – unable to do *anything* without Ryan's approval. Melissa imagined the liberation she felt was akin to a prisoner being released after years in jail. He'd called, texted, sent flowers – begged her to come back; promised he'd change. Now she was out, Melissa couldn't think of anything worse than living with a man who questioned why she was wearing perfume if she went out without him.

Then the anger had come. Calling her a slut and a whore, and didn't she know how lucky she was he'd taken her and Theo in: looked after a child who wasn't his. She should be grateful he'd been willing to look after them both and there weren't many men who'd be so understanding.

It was after he'd text her the message, *Once a slut, always as slut* that she'd decided enough was enough and something drastic needed to happen. She'd called a friend, they'd made a plan and their trip to Barbados had been organised for Christmas. Who knew what would happen at the end of the two weeks? All Melissa knew was she would now have the space and time to think. Something she didn't have while she was constantly worrying about Ryan turning up.

Melissa could quite happily have drunk gin and tonics until she fell asleep. Waking up as they landed at Grantley Adams airport would have been bliss, but that wasn't an option with Theo to look after.

After Charley had brought her the first G&T, Melissa had settled down in her seat and entertained Theo while the rest of the passengers filled in around her. The excited chatter and the clunk of hand luggage being placed into overhead lockers faded around her as she read to Theo.

After a few minutes she became aware people were looking at her and whispers had replaced some of the excited cheeriness.

Where did she get that?

I want a drink.

Melissa quickly finished the rest of her drink and shoved the empty plastic tumbler down between her and Theo's seats. She'd already had enough attention for one flight thanks to the rude snobby lady at the departure gate.

I mean really? At least she's in a different cabin to me, thought Melissa.

Melissa had strapped Theo to her for take-off, which he took great exception to and started whingeing almost immediately. Melissa desperately tried to distract him, but nothing seemed to work and by the time the plane was lifting off the runway he was wailing and covering his ears. She handed him a bottle of milk to try to help pop the pressure, but even with his frantic guzzling, it didn't work.

She could feel each and every passengers' eyes boring into her from behind. She snuggled in to try to comfort her son, studiously avoiding the stares of the passengers to the side of her. Nobody wanted her son to calm down and stop crying more than she did, she was quite sure of that. She hated it when he was upset and there was nothing she could do to soothe him, it made her feel like a failure; like she was a bad mother. Christ knew she'd heard that enough times from Ryan.

As the plane levelled off at 30,000 feet – a fact the pilot had informed them all of before take-off – Theo's wailing calmed down to a sob and then slowly to a whimper. She could feel the pressure of her fellow passengers' judgement lift and the air around her mellowed.

A few minutes later Theo handed the empty milk bottle to Melissa. 'Finished, Mama.'

'Do you feel better now? Do your ears still hurt?'

'No, Mama.' He shook his head emphatically. 'Can get down now?'

'You can sit in your own seat and play, would you like that?'

After settling Theo in his seat with a few toys, Melissa took a moment to herself to gather her thoughts and try to relax.

She had dithered about whether taking a break and travelling so far with a toddler was a good idea, but realising it meant she didn't need to worry about surprise visits from Ryan for a while, she decided to go for it. Right up, that was, until she gathered everything she needed and started trying to load it into the taxi to take them to the airport. From that moment to this, she wished she hadn't bothered. She had to constantly remind herself *why* she was going and that it would all be worth it in the long run.

Melissa tried to block out the hum of the aeroplane engines

and ignore the strange, thin, air-conditioned atmosphere around her. She imagined the warmth of the sun on her skin, the green-blue sea of the Caribbean, the beautiful white sandy beaches, palm trees and amazing sunsets. Yes, it would definitely be worth it in the end. And her friend had told her the Bajan people were incredibly friendly, so maybe getting off at the other side wouldn't be so stressful.

'Would you like a drink, madam?'

'Oh.' The flight attendant was standing right next to her. 'Yes, thank you. Could I have a coffee please?'

'Sure.' He signalled to his colleague. 'It won't be a moment. Would you like a drink for the little one?'

'No, that's okay. I have some drinks and snacks for him.'

'Just let me know if you run out, we have some Fruit Shoots if you need them. Here you go.' He handed her a cup of hot black coffee. 'Milk and sugar?'

'No, thank you.'

The flight attendant smiled and continued on his journey up the aisle.

With Theo content beside her and a warm cup of coffee in her hand, Melissa pulled out her Kindle and settled down to read, taking full advantage of her quiet son.

CHAPTER NINE

MELISSA

Seven and a half hours to landing

A short while later Melissa noticed the cabin crew suddenly seemed busy, hustling through the cabin, speaking quietly, their faces tense. She heard whispers about first class and was certain she heard the word 'doctor' as well. Perhaps someone had taken ill? Whatever had happened, it wasn't any of her concern and she turned her attention back to her book.

After a few minutes the announcement chime sounded and it was as if someone had cast a spell over the people on board. The silence was so immediate it was incredible.

Could anyone with medical training please let themselves be known to the cabin crew, we require your assistance.

The whispering from the passengers started up again as quickly as it had stopped.

Melissa froze. *Oh God no.*

This was her worst nightmare. Yes, she was a nurse, but that was not the same as being a doctor and she was supposed to be on holiday. This was supposed to be a break from constantly *thinking* all of the time. She closed her eyes and prayed there was a doctor on board.

A minute or so later, the chimes sounded again.

Could anyone with medical training please let themselves be known to the cabin crew, we require your assistance.

Melissa badly wanted to stay seated and do nothing; how much could she conceivably do at 30,000 feet anyway. Then she remembered the oath she had sworn on the day she qualified. Ah, who was she kidding – it's not like she hadn't broken it once or twice already.

Melissa turned back to her Kindle, but found she couldn't concentrate and ended up reading the same sentence several times.

After a few minutes, her conscience and curiosity got the better of her and she gave up. Melissa pushed her call bell. She didn't have to wait long for it to be answered.

'Hello, madam.' The attendant raised his eyebrows.

'I'm a nurse – you called for medical help. I mean, I know I'm not a doctor, but I don't think you've had anyone else put their hand up?'

'Oh! No, we haven't. Would you mind coming with me?'

'My son...' Melissa gestured to where Theo sat, watching her curiously.

'Can I get one of the other flight attendants to look after him for a few minutes?'

'Yeah, sure, that's fine.'

Another crew member arrived and Melissa followed Stan, as he had introduced himself, up towards the front of the aircraft. As he led her up the stairs to the upper deck, Melissa gaped at the change in decor around her. The difference between economy and first class was as stark as the difference between a guest house and a five-star hotel, yet there were only a few metres between the two.

As they approached the top of the stairs Melissa's eyes grew wide and she drew in a sharp breath. If she thought the shift in decor going up the stairs was unbelievable, that was nothing compared to what she was looking at in front of her. First class was *poles* apart from economy. Each passenger had their own little cubicle with a much larger TV screen. She could see a little bar of snacks and drinks in each compartment, and they had real glasses and proper pillows too.

She took in the grandeur around her and wondered if she would ever be in a position to be able to afford to sit in first class. As her eyes swept the cabin they fell on a group of familiar-looking people huddled round one of the cubicles; their faces anguished and tear-stained. The sight halted her appraisal and she remembered she'd been asked to help because someone was unwell.

The man who had assisted her with her bag at check-in was the first person she noticed; his tall stature and sandy blond hair were hard to miss – he looked horrified. There was a similarly tall blonde woman clinging to his arm, tears streaming down her face. A thought elbowed its way into Melissa's mind: *She's got to be incredibly uncomfortable dressed like that – even if she is sitting in first class.* Beside her stood Charley, the flight attendant who had been so kind to Melissa earlier.

'We're not sure what's happened, but we are fairly sure she's passed.' Stan spoke quietly in Melissa's ear focusing her attention back on the matter at hand.

Passed? What did they expect her to do? The woman was still in her seat, so clearly no one had attempted CPR and it had been at least ten minutes since the first call for a doctor went out.

Although, if the passenger really was dead, at least Melissa couldn't make it any worse.

Charley spotted her and shot a questioning look at Stan.

'Melissa is a nurse, she's offered to help.'

'Help?' spat the blonde. 'She's dead, how can she *help?*'

The man she clung to turned to face Melissa and a look of recognition passed between them.

'Why don't we all make some space, maybe sit down and let Melissa take a look at Mother?' he said gently.

Mother? It couldn't be...

Melissa swallowed hard and crept forward as the small group parted allowing her a path through. Approaching the seat from behind, as she drew level with the passenger her fears were confirmed – it was the posh lady who had been so rude to her. Melissa's eyes snapped to Charley's face as she remembered what the woman had said to her earlier.

'I can maybe slip a sleeping pill into her pre-flight champagne?'

The flight attendant must have been thinking the same thing: her eyes grew large and she gave a little shake of her head. Melissa couldn't imagine Charley would have done as she suggested, but even mentioning Charley's previous words would have caused her no end of problems.

Melissa's eyes returned to the woman and it was painfully obvious she had died in her seat; her eyes open, but unseeing. Melissa became acutely aware of the pervading silence around her as everyone watched her, waiting for her to do something.

Melissa did as she was trained to do and checked for a pulse – never assume anything. She pressed hard, but could not find even the faintest flicker. Next she leaned over and put her ear close to the woman's mouth – of course there was no breath. She had to check, if for no other reason than the people watching her expected her to do something.

Melissa stood and spoke directly to Charley, unable to look at the woman's family. 'I'm sorry, but she is dead.'

Melissa heard their renewed sobs as she turned and gently closed the dead woman's eyes. The only thing worse than someone staring at you was a *dead* person staring at you.

'I don't know what your protocols are, but do you have a blanket we can place over her for now?'

'Yes, of course. I'll get one.' Charley returned quickly and handed the blanket to Melissa.

Melissa draped it softly over the body of the woman who had caused her to cry just an hour or so earlier and Melissa wondered how she felt about it.

'Do you... can you... can you tell how she died?'

Melissa turned to see the short bald man with the 1970s moustache standing next to her, his eyes on the blanket-covered body of his late wife.

'I'm... was... Vivian's husband.'

'I'm sorry, I'm not very sure. There didn't seem to be any physical symptoms on her body. How was she just before she...'

'She kept rubbing at her head and neck, like she had a headache, and her breathing was all funny.'

'Did you notice if she had any pain in her chest, or her arms?'

'Do you think it was a heart attack then?'

'It does sound like it.'

'But you're not a doctor are you?' The cut-glass accent of the model-like blonde commanded her attention.

'No, I'm a nurse–'

'So you really don't know what happened, you're guessing.'

'Um, I suppose you'd call it an educated guess–'

'A guess? What use is that? I think she took an overdose.'

An overdose?

The younger man gasped. 'What makes you think that? Why would Mother want to take her own life?'

The blonde turned to the man next to her. 'I'm not saying it was deliberate. Aaron, I saw her take one of those awful powdered painkillers we kept telling her to stop taking, but I know she took at least one just before we left the lounge. I wonder if she lost track and ended up taking too many by accident.'

'I really don't see—'

'It was a few minutes after that she started gasping for breath. It's got to be linked.'

'That does seem rather unlikely, Lydia. I think Melissa is probably right, she's had a heart attack, nothing more sinister than that,' said Aaron.

If help had been summoned as soon as she had started having symptoms, Melissa may have been able to do something more than just check for a pulse. But telling them that wasn't going to help anyone and the last thing she wanted to do was cause them any further anguish.

A short woman with an elegant grey bob spoke. 'What happens now?'

'It's simple, they'll have to turn the plane around, won't they? We're not that far from Heathrow, so it makes sense.'

'Of course they will. We can't fly all the way to Barbados with a *corpse* on board.' Lydia shuddered.

Aaron turned to look at the woman aghast.

'Oh, I'm sorry, Aaron, I didn't mean to be insensitive, but the thought of sharing a cabin with a dead body gives me the creeps – even if she is your mother.'

Aaron shook his head and turned to Charley. 'Is that right? Do we turn the plane around?'

'I need to go and alert the pilots as to what's happened. I'll know more once I've spoken to them.'

49

'Okay. Melissa?' He looked at her kindly. 'Thank you for your assistance.'

'I didn't really do anything.'

'I know, but you tried.'

'I'm very sorry for your loss.' Melissa smiled sadly. 'If you don't need me anymore, I'd better get back to my son.'

'Of course,' said Charley. 'I'll go and speak to the pilot now.'

CHAPTER TEN

CHARLEY

Letting out a loud breath, Charley squared her shoulders and made her way downstairs and to the front of the aircraft.

'You okay?' asked her colleague, Jen.

'I'm fine. I've just never had to deal with anything like this before?' Charley slumped against the bulkhead now she was out of sight of the passengers. She wanted nothing more than to neck a brandy, but to do so in front of a rookie would be seriously unprofessional. 'I don't supposed you have either?'

'No. Anything I can do to help?'

'Could you go up and see if the wedding party need anything while I speak to Liz and let her know what's going on?'

'Of course,' she replied a little nervously.

'We've covered her with a blanket, don't worry.' Charley realised she'd spoken to the young woman a little too harshly, but before she could apologise, Jen had simply nodded and left.

Despite having been long-haul cabin crew for more than fifteen years, Charley had never had someone die on board. She'd never even had a medical emergency – the worst thing that had ever happened was a nose bleed that wouldn't stop.

They were trained in a kind of advanced first aid, but Charley knew, despite not being a doctor, there was nothing that could be done for the woman by the time the alarm had been raised.

She rubbed her forehead. She didn't have a clue what the proper protocol was. She was fairly certain they wouldn't be turning around, but what was she supposed to do with the body? Surely they couldn't leave her where she was, it wouldn't be fair on the rest of the passengers. But where else would they put her? Economy was full.

Liz would know. Charley headed for the flight deck door and picked up the intercom handset.

'Liz? It's Charley.'

'Hey, Charley, how's it going back there?'

'Not great, we've got a bit of a situation actually.'

'What kind of situation?'

Charley could hear the change in the pilot's tone; friendliness turned to businesslike in a second.

'One of the passengers in first class has passed away, looks like a heart attack.' Charley wondered whether she ought to mention the suspected overdose, but decided against it. The rest of the family had dismissed the suggestion.

'Oh shit. Family on board?'

'Yeah, it's the mother of the groom from the wedding party.'

'That sucks. Where is she?'

'Still in her seat with a blanket over her. To be honest, Liz, I'm not really sure what I'm doing. I've never had a death on board before.'

'Unfortunately, the only spare seat is in first class, so she'll need to stay where she is until we get to our destination. I'll radio and let ground control know the situation.'

'I take it we're not turning around then?'

'No, there's no point. Sad as it is, there's nothing can be done

for the poor woman and we have an aeroplane full of other passengers expecting to go on holiday.'

'That's what I thought you'd say.' Charley sighed. 'The family aren't the type to take it well.'

'They never do. Just give them the official line that we're still way overweight to land and we'd have to fly in circles for hours to use up fuel anyway. Which is all true, incidentally. If they get really shitty, give me a shout and I can come and speak to them for a few minutes.'

'Thanks, Liz. I'll bear it in mind as a last resort. Right, I'd better go and give them the good news.'

'Good luck!'

Charley hung up the intercom and leaned against the wall. As cabin crew you knew there was always a chance something like this might happen. If anything, she'd been incredibly lucky it hadn't happened before, but of all the families, of course it had to be this one.

As soon as they'd got on board she knew they were going to be difficult. The rude and dismissive way they treated everyone around them made that obvious. It was clear they thought of her and her colleagues as nothing more than waitresses, only there to answer their every beck and call. And there was no doubt they were used to getting their own way, telling them the aeroplane would be carrying on to Barbados as planned was not going to go down well.

Realising she couldn't put it off much longer, Charley stood and straightened her uniform.

'They're asking what's going on,' said Jen, reappearing.

'I'm just coming. We'll be flying on to Barbados and the body will need to stay where it is, we've nowhere else to put it.'

Jen shook her head. 'Oh they're gonna love that.'

'I know. I was preparing myself for the backlash.'

'I don't blame you. I'll come too, we'll present a united front.'

'Thanks.'

Charley slowly made her way back up the stairs as if trying to prevent the inevitable. Once she reached the top, she took a deep breath, swept aside the curtain and entered the proverbial lions' den.

As Charley entered the cabin, she took stock of the scene before her. The bride's parents were sitting in their seats, their heads close together, deep in conversation. Mr Grant-Fernsby noticed her arrival and nudged his wife, raising his chin in Charley's direction. At his gesture, his wife turned to look at her as well.

Rex Fortescue was standing beside his son, and his daughter-in-law-to-be was sitting in her seat, her face red and a shredded tissue clutched in her hand. How did some women still manage to look beautiful when they had been crying? The only kind of crying Charley had ever been capable of was the ugly kind.

'Mr Fortescue?'

'Yes?' Aaron and Rex answered quickly.

'Apologies, may I call you both by your first name to avoid any confusion?'

'Of course.' Aaron cut his father off as he opened his mouth. 'I'm Aaron and this is my father, Rex.'

The look Rex gave his son was not lost on Charley. He clearly thought of himself as the head of the family and was put out by Aaron answering on their behalf.

'Is the pilot turning the plane around?' Rex's attempt to regain some of the power was feeble at best.

'I have spoken with the pilot and she has decided that we will not be doing s–'

'That is unacceptable,' Rex bellowed, his face red.

Alcohol or anger? Charley wondered.

'I demand this plane returns to London immediately. We cannot possibly fly for another seven hours with my wife's body on board. Not only is it completely inappropriate, it is downright demeaning to my late wife.'

Charley found it interesting that the man had so quickly started referring to his wife as 'late'. She opened her mouth to explain the situation, but before she could say a word, Aaron Fortescue was already speaking.

'Dad,' the warning in his tone was unmistakable, 'I think we should let...'

'Charley, my name's Charley.'

'Charley explain the captain's decision before we start shouting and making demands.'

Rex stared hard at his son. 'Fine.'

Rex Fortescue was behaving like a petulant child and despite Vivian's earlier rudeness, Charley was beginning to wonder what the woman had seen in him. Rude she may have been, but there was at least a pretence of class and upbringing, even if her behaviour contradicted it.

She nodded a thank you in Aaron's direction and continued.

'As I was saying, the captain has decided we will be continuing to Barbados. There are several reasons for this, the most important is fuel. We have too much fuel on board to land at the moment, and if we did head back to Heathrow, we would only end up circling for several hours to burn off enough to allow us to land. There are also the remaining passengers to take into consideration. Whilst I have no doubt they would all be extremely upset by what has happened, they would want to continue with their holidays as planned.'

'What about *us*? What about what we want? We are grieving and my wife's body deserves respect.'

Again, Charley was struck by the man's choice of words. Grieving seemed like such an odd thing to say so quickly.

'I think what my father is trying to say is, we would like my mother to be looked after as soon as possible.'

'Of course, I completely understand. This is the quickest way to have her appropriately taken care of. The captain will radio ahead and alert ground control as to what has happened. Someone will meet you at the airport and guide you through your next steps.'

'It doesn't sound like the pilot is going to change her mind, but I must say I'm not terribly happy,' said Aaron.

'I appreciate that, sir, but this really is standard procedure.'

'Standard procedure, my arse!'

It took Charley a moment to understand who was speaking. Rex Fortescue's voice had changed from something akin to a middle-class English non-accent to pure Scots. Startled, Charley staggered as the man pushed past her and ran down the stairs.

By the time she had caught up with him, the newly-made widower was banging on the cockpit door.

'I demand you turn this plane around! Let me in!'

Charley placed a hand on Rex's shoulder. 'Mr Fortescue.'

'Don't touch me.' Rex whirled round as he spoke and swiped Charley's hand away.

She stumbled slightly and fell against the wall of the plane.

'Dad!'

Rex's eyes blazed; somehow he seemed taller and wider.

'Open this door, now.' His voice had turned into a pure guttural growl.

'Dad, stop.'

Aaron had placed himself between his father and Charley, allowing her the time and space to stand up properly. She smoothed down her uniform, and moved away, putting some distance, and Aaron, between her and the older man.

Yes this family had suffered a dreadful loss under difficult circumstances, but she would not, could not, allow a passenger to think they could do whatever they wanted. What if he assaulted one of the other cabin crew? One of the *passengers*? Very quickly this flight could go from bad to worse and she needed to curtail that behaviour – now.

'Mr Fortescue.' Charley's tone was hard and she made sure it left the man under no illusions as to who was actually in charge. 'I must ask you to desist from this behaviour. You are achieving nothing and if you continue I will have no choice but to instruct the captain to ensure law enforcement is waiting on the ground for our arrival. That door cannot be opened from this side and given your current behaviour there is absolutely no way either of the pilots are going to allow you, or me, entry. I must ask you to return to your seat immediately and avoid any further upset.'

Rex's eyes were wild and his breathing came in short bursts. Charley desperately wanted to look to his son for assistance, but knew looking away would make her appear weak.

'Charley? Is everything okay?'

'Mr Fortescue was just returning to his seat, Stan,' said Charley, still not breaking eye contact.

The physical change in Rex's stature was obvious; his shoulders turned inwards and he lowered his eyes.

'Of course, I apologise. I let my emotions get the better of me.' The plummy English accent had returned.

'I quite understand, Mr Fortescue.'

'Go and sit down, Dad, I'll be there in a minute. I'll see if these lovely people might be able to rustle us up some tea, shall I?'

Rex clapped Aaron on the shoulder and looked like he was trying desperately not to cry. 'Thanks, son.'

Charley, Stan and Aaron watched as Rex made his way

slowly towards the staircase, his eyes never leaving the ground. And who could blame him with the passengers in economy staring at him so openly.

'I'll organise you all some tea and I'm sure we have some biscuits. The sugar will be good for the shock.'

'Thank you. I'm sorry about my father...' Aaron trailed off, apparently not sure what excuses to make.

'That's quite all right and as long as there are no other incidents, we'll forget about it.'

'You're very kind. You're not injured?'

'No, not at all, just a bit of a surprise.'

'As long as he didn't hurt you.' Aaron turned to go back to his seat, but instead slumped against the bulkhead.

'Sir? Are you okay?' Charley placed a hand on his shoulder. She felt sorry for him; his mother had died and his father was being no father at all. It was as if the two men had reversed roles.

'I'm a little in shock to be honest. Do you think I might be able to have a brandy?'

'Of course, let me get that for you.'

Charley pulled open various drawers and, having found a miniature, fixed the drink and handed it to Aaron. He tipped the glass up and swallowed it in one mouthful. Colour appeared in his cheeks a few moments later.

He handed her back the glass. 'Thank you,' he said with a watery smile. 'I believe that might have done the trick.'

'You're welcome.' Charley found herself unable to look away from his sad blue eyes. She wanted to hug him and tell him it would all be okay. Tell him he would be better off without his vile mother, but of course she didn't; couldn't.

Aaron rubbed his hand on his jeans. 'I'd better go and check...'

'Yes.'

'The tea?'

'I'll make sure someone brings it.'

'Thank you. By the way, what will happen to Mother now? I mean, for the rest of the flight?'

'I'm afraid we'll need to keep Mrs Fortescue where she is, covered with the blanket. We simply have nowhere else to put her.'

'Of course, I understand.'

The younger Mr Fortescue finally made his way back to his seat.

Charley felt terrible for him, not only had his mother just died suddenly, he clearly felt himself responsible for his father's behaviour too.

Stan appeared in Aaron's place.

'Stan, could you organise some tea and biscuits please? And maybe just check the rest of the passengers are okay? Actually, it wouldn't do any harm for us to reassure them, I think they must have heard about what's going on. I'm going to update Liz.'

'Sure thing.'

Charley picked up the intercom phone and waited for her captain to answer.

'*Everything okay out there?*' Liz sounded worried.

'Everything's fine now. Mr Fortescue Senior wasn't happy with your decision to continue on to Barbados. He thought he would take it upon himself to urge you to change your mind.' Charley chuckled at just how ridiculous that sounded.

'*Ha! As if that would ever happen. I'm guessing you disabused him of that notion?*'

'I did, he's now sitting in his seat like a model passenger and awaiting his tea and biscuits.'

'*Excellent work,*' said Liz with a laugh. '*You okay though? You sound a bit shaky.*'

'Yeah, I *am* a bit shaky but I'm fine. It was weird, he flicked from this middle-class posh bloke into an aggressive man with a strong Scottish accent. Threw me a bit, that's all.'

'If he starts anything else, we'll have to detain him. You just say the word.'

'I think he'll be okay now. His son seems to have some sway over him.'

Charley replaced the handset and hoped that would be an end to any eventfulness and things could return to how they would normally run.

With the exception of a dead body on board, of course.

CHAPTER ELEVEN

AARON

'Hey, dude, you okay?'

Aaron felt a hand on his shoulder and looked up to see sad brown eyes looking down on him. Darius. He'd barely given his friend a second thought since they boarded the plane. Between trying to stop his mother alienating everyone, her *death* – God! – and his father's outburst, Aaron hadn't had the head space for anything else.

He gripped Darius's hand in place on his shoulder. 'I-I'm fine.'

'You sure? Because we can go and get a drink in the bar if you want?'

Aaron considered it for a moment. 'Yeah, let's do that.'

He turned to speak to Lydia, but she looked to have fallen asleep with her headphones on watching a film. She'd figure it out – there weren't many places he could be.

As soon as they entered the bar Aaron realised he'd done the right thing. The cabin, despite the individual seat areas and extra space, had felt oppressive. He hadn't expected the bar to offer a reprieve from that, but the lack of uniformed seating meant that it did. They could move around and it felt freer, less claustrophobic and since there were no other passengers in first class, they had the place to themselves.

The semi-circular bar stood in the middle of the plane with a curtain either side which led back to the first class cabin. There were tubes of gently glowing lights at floor level, not only around the bar, but also around the plush bench seats.

Everywhere Aaron looked there were lights and lamps, but somehow the bar area was not overly bright. Whoever had designed it had done so with perfect taste and skill. The soft light seemed to tone down, take the edge off, the horror that had occurred not an hour earlier.

Despite it being compact, the bar looked to be incredibly well stocked and there were small plates of snack foods dotted around the place. Aaron reflected that in a parallel universe, not only would his mother still be alive, but he would most likely have spent the majority of the flight in here. His first class seat was comfortable, of that there was no doubt, but a man would have no choice but to relax, take a load off and enjoy the hospitality once here.

'Dude, you want a whisky? Brandy?'

'Since when have I ever drunk whisky?' His tone was light.

'Yeah, yeah, I know, but I thought maybe for the shock?'

Aaron gave him a look that said, *don't be a weirdo*. 'I'll just have a beer. No point in ending up hammered.'

'True. Especially not when–' Darius cut himself off.

Aaron looked up sharply. 'Not when what?'

'It's nothing. Ignore me. I shouldn't have said anything.' Darius pulled a bottle of sanitiser from his pocket and squirted some onto his hand.

'Yeah, but you did. So now you have to tell me. And by the way, your obsession with germs and hand sanitiser is fucking unhealthy.' Aaron could feel irritation prodding at him. The hand sanitiser thing was a cheap shot, but he felt it justified. Why was Darius poking the bear now?

'I only meant that with your pop's getting a bit... confrontational, it's probably a good idea to keep a clear head.'

'Confrontational? Is that what we're calling it? He tried to force his way into the cockpit and then shoved a woman into the wall. He was violent and aggressive, and I'm embarrassed by his behaviour. So yes, you're right, part of the reason I don't want to get drunk is because I feel like I need to protect people from my own father!'

The air steward behind the bar turned away, suddenly intrigued by something behind him.

Darius blanched slightly, looking like Aaron had just kicked his cat.

Aaron took a step back and leaned forwards on the bar heavily, his arms straight and his eyes closed. He stood upright and took a deep breath. Opening his eyes he turned to Darius. 'I'm sorry, that was completely uncalled for.'

'It's okay, man, I get it,' said Darius with a faint smile.

'You're a good friend, Darius, better than I deserve.'

'Now you're just being stupid. I love you, man, you know that.'

'I do.' Aaron squeezed his friend's shoulder.

Darius held Aaron's gaze for a few seconds and Aaron began to feel uncomfortable. He averted his eyes, looking for his drink, which he found and took a long pull.

'I don't think I can do this, you know.'

'Of course you can, I'll help you. These people know what they're doing and when we get to Barbados there will be people there who deal with this stuff all the time.'

'What are you talking about?'

'What are *you* talking about?'

'*I'm...*' Aaron looked around but there was only the flight attendant there. 'About marrying Lydia. I don't think I love her enough and I don't think she loves me.'

'Oh, I thought you meant having to deal with getting your mum back to the UK and your dad and stuff. Surely this... situation,' Darius wafted his hand around in the air, '... is the perfect excuse. You tell her you can't possibly get married now, under the circumstances.'

'You mean let her down gently when we get back?'

'Yeah, something like that. But, dude, I still don't get why you asked her in the first place?'

'You know why, everyone told me to and it seemed like a good way to get people off my back. It's not like she'd be a terrible wife.'

Darius shook his head. 'People don't get married to people who might make a good wife or a good husband anymore. I mean, damn, just how old fashioned are your family? And anyway, if you were happy to settle before, what's changed now?'

'You know what.'

'Yeah, but you made a decision. Are you telling me you've changed your mind?'

'I have – especially now.' Aaron's eyes locked on Darius's. Aaron looked away and picked at the label on his beer bottle, needing to give his hands something to do.

When Darius didn't say anything Aaron looked up and saw a strange look on his friend's face. 'Don't look at me like that. It's not something I can help. I met her years ago and then bumped into her again recently and realised just how much I love her. You know this. I've *never* felt like this about Lydia. I don't want to hurt either of them. God! This is such a mess!'

Darius's expression had changed and Aaron was struggling to understand what his friend was thinking.

Darius lay his hand on Aaron's arm. 'I'm not judging you, I

promise. You've just always been so... straight. I want you to be sure you're doing the right thing either way.'

'Straight? Really? That's the word you choose to describe me?' Aaron quirked his eyebrow and a smile played on his lips.

'You know what I mean.' Darius punched him on the shoulder playfully. 'Seriously though, if you truly love this woman then you know what you have to do. It'll be hard, no doubt about it, but you can't marry Lydia out of some weird sense of loyalty or some bullshit like that. You, Lydia and this other woman all deserve more. I'm here though. You know I'll do whatever you need me to.'

'Thank you, I appreciate it.'

'Now you just have to get back to the UK without being forced down the aisle by bridezilla!'

Aaron groaned, Darius chuckled, and they went back to their drinks.

CHAPTER TWELVE

LYDIA

Six and a half hours to landing

Lydia woke with a start, the film she had been watching was halfway through and she only remembered seeing the first ten minutes or so. The recent sleepless nights and the stress of organising a destination wedding had taken their toll. Still, it wouldn't be long before it was all over.

She saw Vivian's blanket-covered body and the events of their journey so far came rushing back to Lydia with startling clarity. Vivian was dead. Now there would be the added stress of having her body repatriated to the UK, and a funeral to organise. This was absolutely the last thing Lydia needed.

Lydia took a few moments to cast her eyes around the rest of the cabin. Her mother and father were in their seats and she assumed Aaron and Darius were in the bar. Rex appeared to have stopped chuntering and she was relieved he wasn't annoying anyone.

Her eyes flicked back to Vivian's seat, and although she

couldn't see the woman, she was acutely aware she was now sharing space with a dead body; the thought made it feel like there were woodlice marching across her arms.

Her mother-in-law's death was both shocking and sad, but Lydia couldn't help but think of the ways it benefited her. The Fortescue's were the kind of people who wrote wills – they had to, such was their wealth – so there was no doubt there would be something coming Aaron's way, but the rest would unquestionably go to Rex.

Think how wealthy we would be if Rex died too?

Lydia felt only a moment's guilt for wishing ill of her father-in-law. She wasn't generally the kind of person who wanted people dead, but sometimes their absence would make life easier for those left behind. And anyway, Rex wasn't one of them, not really. It didn't matter how many elocution lessons he took, or how Vivian dressed him up like a Ken doll, he was still just a working class nobody from the east end of Glasgow. A subject that was never discussed, but was also one of the worst-kept secrets around.

Lydia's stomach gurgled and her eyes widened as she sat upright. She breathed deeply to try to quell the rising nausea. Spending eight hours in the toilet was not quite how she envisaged the flight to her wedding.

'Are you okay, honey?' Aaron had returned from the bar, a concerned expression on his face.

She ignored his sympathy as she climbed from her seat and raced towards the toilet, grateful it was vacant, and that it was larger than the average aeroplane toilet cubical. Once inside she managed to seat herself with not a second to spare and prayed there was no one waiting outside to hear her.

Moments later, the sickness started and she had no choice but to aim towards the sink and hope it all made it in there. At this stage, Lydia had learned from experience, there was nothing to do but let it run its course.

She'd been ill for a couple of weeks, but had managed to downplay how bad it was in front of her family. Lydia did not like to be fussed over when she was ill, and she knew if her mother, or Aaron, knew about the pins and needles, or how weak she felt, there would be no end to the fussing and faffing she would have to endure.

She was certain the weakness was due to the sickness and likely the sleeplessness she'd lived with recently. The latter she was sure would soon disappear once they had landed in Barbados and she and Aaron were married. It was likely stress; God knew she'd been under enough of it.

It was a well-known fact organising a wedding was stressful and insomnia was just a symptom of that. Her anxiety had not been helped by the fact Vivian wanted to be included on every decision and if she didn't deem it 'proper' or classy enough then it had to go – no matter what Lydia and Aaron wanted. Lydia had been more than prepared to fight her, but Aaron had begged her to play nice and take into consideration that he was her only child and she would have no daughters' weddings to organise.

Lydia had agreed, but put her foot down when Vivian tried to force her into a godawful, frumpy, frilly wedding dress because it was more *demure*. Instead Lydia had opted for a champagne coloured, figure-skimming fishtail dress with simple straps and zero fuss. It screamed elegance and therefore money, which was how she persuaded her mother-in-law it was the right dress to go for.

She's not even going to be there now. What a waste of time.

Still there were a few things that could be changed to suit Lydia now that Vivian was no longer able to cast disapproving looks over everything.

The more Lydia thought about it, the more she realised that

would also be the case when they arrived home from their honeymoon. She would be able to decorate any way she chose. She could drive any car she wished and could frequent any restaurant she wished. Lydia had planned to do all these things anyway, but now there would be no pointed looks or barbed comments and Aaron would not have to play peacekeeper.

A gentle knocking on the door accompanied her mother's voice. 'Lydia, darling, are you all right in there?'

'Yes, Mother, just a moment.' Lydia forced levity into her tone, all the while rolling her eyes.

She made a half-hearted attempt to clean up around her before deciding they'd paid enough for her air fare and someone else could finish the job.

Lydia opened the door to find her mother still standing on the other side. Thankfully, there was no one else around.

'There you are,' said Daphne Grant-Fernsby, peering at her daughter. 'You do look awfully pale...'

'I really do wish everyone would stop fussing – and talking about my health. It's embarrassing enough for me knowing people see every time I have to rush to the bathroom without everyone constantly asking me if I'm okay. I'd really rather not bring any more attention to it.'

'I'm sorry, dear, we're just a bit concerned that's all. Look, I know what you said to Vivian, but you can tell me, are you sure you're not pregnant?'

Lydia groaned. 'Yes, Mother, I'm sure I'm not pregnant.'

'Because you know it would be quite fortuitous given our current–'

'I'm quite aware of that, there is no need to mention it every time we speak. I know what is expected of me and I am doing my part, but I will do it my way.' Lydia glanced around. 'This really isn't the time or the place to be having this discussion anyway, anyone could creep up or overhear.'

'I really don't think there's any need to speak to me like that, Lydia. I only have the best interests of this family at heart.' Daphne stalked back to her seat.

Lydia returned to her own seat and sat. Aaron opened his mouth, but before he could say anything, she held up her hand. 'I'm fine, please don't fuss.'

'Wouldn't dream of it,' he replied, holding up both hands defensively.

'There are a few things we need to sort out when we get to the hotel before the wedding. We need to finalise the flower choices and also, apparently there is a problem with the menu. I said we'd deal with it once we were there.'

Aaron's expression morphed into one of confusion.

'You never listen to me, do you? I did tell you about this before we left,' said Lydia, her tone tight.

'I do listen and I remember you telling me, but you can't seriously think we're going to get married now? My mother's just died and you're still expecting us to get married in three days?'

Lydia hadn't even considered that they might postpone the wedding, but she could see now how it might look if they got married within a few days of a family bereavement.

'Of course we can postpone. We'll speak to the wedding planner and see if we can't push it back to after the weekend.'

'What? No, as soon as we can I'll be having Mother's body flown back to the UK. We'll still get married, we'll just have to rethink the when and the where.'

Lydia was starting to panic; this was not in the plan. Somehow she was going to have to convince Aaron to go ahead with the wedding.

'It just seems like a terrible waste of money for us to fly our friends to a gorgeous Caribbean island and then *not* get married. I understand you might not want to do it straight away, and it might be a more sombre occasion than we'd planned, but I don't see any reason not to do it. It's not like your mother will be able to attend at a later date anyway.' Lydia realised her mistake as soon as the words left her mouth.

'I can't believe you've just said that. My mother isn't even cold yet and you come out with something so insensitive.'

'Aaron, I'm s–'

'Please don't say any more. I'd like to be left alone for a while.'

Lydia watched as Aaron plugged in his headphones and began tapping at his screen.

'The flight attendant thought you might like some water,' said Rex offering her a bottle.

'Thank you.' Lydia took the bottle and flopped back in her seat. She sent her mind into overdrive trying to find a way to persuade Aaron to change his mind.

She had no other choice.

CHAPTER THIRTEEN

MELISSA

Six hours to landing

All around Melissa the whispers had died down and the other passengers had gone back to whatever it was they did to pass their time in the air.

When she had arrived back at her seat, Theo was curled up in a ball and fast asleep. Melissa covered him with a blanket and dropped a gentle kiss on his forehead, wondering *how* she was going to get her little boy to sleep at the right time once they arrived in the Caribbean, but that was a problem for later. She was grateful he was sleeping now so she could concentrate on her thoughts.

Had the old woman taken an overdose? And if she had, why now? Why here, somewhere above the middle of the Atlantic? Melissa mulled the idea in her mind – considered the appearance of the body and the information she had been given by the rest of the family. Everything seemed to point to a heart attack, but the fact the woman had been seen taking a powdered painkiller moments before her death and not long before the flight, niggled at Melissa.

Who even took powdered painkillers anymore? And who took them in the manner described to her? Melissa couldn't think of anything worse – the dry powder poured into your mouth and then washed down with a swig of water. Eugh! She shuddered at the thought.

Could Vivian have been allergic to the powders? Unlikely, since Lydia had said she took them often. Maybe they changed the ingredients? Who knew?

More to the point, why was Melissa spending her time worrying about it? There was nothing she could do from up here and it wasn't even her job on the ground. She much preferred to work with living patients – and preferably grateful ones, which Vivian Fortescue most likely would not have been. Melissa reminded herself how rude the woman had been just a few short hours before, not once, but twice. And the second time was in front of a group of strangers where she had reduced Melissa to tears.

Satisfied that she did not need to concern herself with Vivian Fortescue's demise, or have any further unnecessary contact with her family, Melissa called for a member of cabin crew and searched for a film to watch while she waited.

'Did you call?'

'Oh, yes, thank you.' Why did they have to sneak up like that? 'Could I possibly have a coffee and a bottle of water please?'

'Sure, anything else? We still have some hot meals left, I think you missed yours while you were helping us out.'

'A hot meal would be great, thank you.'

'Coming right up.'

Melissa pulled out her tray in readiness for her refreshments and plugged in her headphones. An oldie but a goodie, she pressed play on *Pretty Woman* and settled in for what she hoped would be a quiet couple of hours.

A few minutes later she was tucking into chicken and potatoes in a creamy white wine sauce. It wasn't bad for aeroplane food.

Once she had finished she settled back into her seat and felt her eyes start to close as she drifted off listening to 'King of Wishful Thinking'.

Melissa awoke to her name being stage-whispered in her ear and someone shaking her arm. She jolted upright and immediately looked for Theo; he was still asleep in the seat beside her. She looked at her watch – she'd been asleep for half an hour – and then looked for the person who had shaken her awake.

Charley.

'Sorry, I didn't mean to startle you,' she said, wincing slightly.

'It's fine.' Melissa rubbed her face and then took out her earphones. 'What's up? Don't tell me there's another body.'

Charley held on to the back of the seat to steady herself. 'How could you know that?'

'What? I was joking.' Melissa stared at the other woman. 'Are you telling me someone else has died?'

'Shh!' Charley glanced around her. 'I don't want the other passengers to hear.'

'Dear God! What happened this time?'

'I'm not sure – I don't think it's a heart attack though.'

'What makes you say that?'

'She's too young. It's Lydia Grant-Fernsby.'

'The bride?'

'Yes. She had an upset tummy, but otherwise seemed fine. Her parents and in-laws-to-be were convinced she was pregnant – she was adamant she wasn't. She had an argument with her fiancé and they both fell asleep. When he woke up he saw how pale she was and tried to wake her. That was the first anyone realised there was something wrong.'

'How awful!'

'Will you come and have a look?'

'Why? If she's dead, like before, there's nothing I can do.' Melissa really did not want to become any more wrapped up in anyone else's problems if she could possibly help it. And there really was nothing she could do.

'I know, but you're the only person here who has any sort of medical training and there's some weird stuff about the body.'

Weird stuff? Melissa really did not want to get involved in any weird stuff. She just wanted to enjoy what she could of the flight and look forward to her holiday in Barbados. A holiday she and Theo very much deserved after their recent spate of bad luck.

'Please? I know this is a lot to ask and I wouldn't normally, but I'm sure there's something suspicious going on. I've never had anyone die on board and now I have two dead bodies, and one of them was a healthy young woman.'

'It sounds like you need a detective, not a nurse.'

'I've been asking around, there aren't any on board.'

Melissa eyed her sceptically. 'Fine. I'll come and take a look, but you have to keep the dad away from me – I don't trust him.'

'Yes! Thank you. He won't be a problem, I promise, he and I have a deal.'

Melissa wondered what kind of deal a flight attendant could

have with a passenger in those sorts of terms and then decided she didn't want to know.

She followed Charley back down the aisle towards the stairs to first class and ignored the watchful eyes of the other passengers. Nosey gits the lot of them.

Once she entered the cabin, the scene before Melissa was all too familiar. This time though, the bride-to-be's mother and father were utterly distraught. Tears poured down Daphne Grant-Fernsby's cheeks, and welled in her husband's eyes – he was clearly doing his damnedest not to cry.

What kind of man tries to keep a stiff upper lip when his child has just died? thought Melissa.

Aaron was standing off to one side and was being consoled by another man – a friend? Rex was standing close by, his face ashen.

Someone had already covered Lydia's body and Melissa wondered for a moment why someone hadn't placed the two women side by side. A second later she realised what a ludicrous thought that would be at any other time, let alone on board an aeroplane somewhere over the Atlantic Ocean.

'Melissa?'

Hearing Charley say her name, Melissa switched her focus back to the here and now.

'I'll just double-check, you know...'

Charley nodded and pulled the blanket from Lydia's face. It was clear she was dead without Melissa even having to touch her, but her professionalism kicked in and she had to confirm the woman's death.

Melissa held the first two fingers of her right hand to Lydia's neck for ten seconds. It was longer than was necessary, but she didn't want there to be any doubt in her mind. There was no pulse to be felt. Withdrawing her fingers she shook her head. 'I'm sorry.'

Someone wailed loudly; the woman's mother. Across the seats, in the other aisle, Melissa could see Aaron trying and failing to keep his emotions in check. After a moment or two, he gave in and the tears ran down his cheeks.

'No, no, no, Lydia. Please God, no.' His words came out in sobs, barely understandable as emotion overwhelmed him.

'Come on, sit down here.' The man supporting him eased him down into the empty seat beside him. Aaron's eyes did not once leave his fiancée's body.

'What do you think?' Charley whispered near Melissa's shoulder.

'Hang on.'

Melissa took hold of the dead girl's hand and inspected it closely. Next she raised each of her eyelids in turn; she wasn't entirely sure what she was looking for. She placed her fingers on the woman's skull, through her hair and probed, again, not knowing what she was expecting to find, but a couple of things struck her as odd.

Melissa stepped back after covering Lydia's body. She didn't want to subject the corpse to any further scrutiny in such a public setting.

'Do you think he'll be able to answer a couple of questions for me?' she asked, watching Aaron trying to control himself.

'Why? Have you found something?' Charley asked.

'Maybe, in fact, I think so, but he might be able to confirm it.'

'Let's go and ask him then. We'll go into the bar, give us a bit of privacy.'

Melissa made her way to the bar as Charley suggested and waited as the flight attendant spoke with the bereaved man who had lost his mother and fiancée in the space of a couple of hours. Melissa watched through the gap in the curtains and although she couldn't make out what they were saying, she could see him shake his head and dig the heels of his hands into his eyes.

Eventually, Melissa saw his shoulders slump and he rose to his feet. She stepped back from the curtain, for some reason not wanting to be caught watching.

'I'm so sorry for your loss,' Melissa offered, wincing as she realised just how feeble that sounded.

'Thank you. Charley says you wanted to ask me some questions?' Aaron visibly tried to pull himself together.

'Yes, can you tell me how long Lydia has been losing her hair for?'

Aaron's focus snapped to Melissa; it felt like his eyes were trying to look inside her head.

'What do you mean? Lydia wasn't losing her hair. Trust me, if she had been I would have known all about it – she would have been constantly complaining.'

'I'm really sorry, but I've just examined her and she definitely had some hair loss. Could she have been hiding it from you?'

'I suppose, but...' Aaron was clearly bewildered. 'Why were you examining her anyway? I know you double-checked her pulse, but what possible reason could you have for examining her body?' Aaron's tone was even, but filled with menace and his eyes flashed at Melissa.

'Um...' She glanced at Charley, not really sure what to say. He'd been there while she'd carried out her examination, why question her now? She swallowed hard and tried to explain it in sympathetic terms – terms that would not anger him further.

'I asked her to.'

Melissa's shoulders dropped, relieved Charley had come to her rescue.

'Why would you do that?' Aaron snapped at Charley.

'Your fiancée has been dashing to the toilet for most of the flight, Mr Fortescue. I also noticed there were some white lines on her fingernails. It struck me as odd, so I asked Melissa to help me. She's the only person on board with any real medical training.'

Aaron turned his attention back to Melissa. 'So what do you think?'

CHAPTER FOURTEEN

The means by which a poison ends up in a person's body depends entirely upon the poison in question. Bearing that in mind, there are four ways to administer poisons: ingestion, respiration, absorption or injection. And just like some poisons are better equipped for the job than others, some administrations prove to be a better vehicle than others. Gas is great, but it's far less selective in who it kills. I mean, if you're into mass murder (I'm looking at you, Hitler) it's perfect, but it's also far more likely to get you caught. And although injection is person-particular, they're likely to notice you jabbing a needle into them.

By far the easiest mechanisms are absorption through the skin and mixing with food and drink for ingestion. They're specific, straightforward and best of all, you can be nowhere near the victim at the time of their death.

The way different poisons behave within the body are varied. Some interrupt communications between cells and nerves which can mean the muscles around the heart aren't told to beat, or the signals to the diaphragm are interrupted and the victim essentially chokes to death. Some poisons pretend to be something else and are allowed entry into cells. Once there they do not perform the job the cell thought they were supposed to and the machinery simply stops working. No cells, no life.

It never ceases to amaze me how few people realise how easy it is to obtain poison. And I don't just mean bleach from the cupboard under the sink or pesticides from the garden shed. Those kinds of poisons are vulgar, obtuse and lack finesse in my opinion. However, sometimes needs must.

My favourite sources of poison are those from everyday items. Items you'd most likely have in your fridge or pantry. Things you would *eat* and not even give a second thought to.

For example, did you know that apple seeds contain cyanide? Don't worry though, you'd have to crunch your way through such vast quantities you'd notice before you came to any harm. This little nugget of information is what teaches us that *dose* is also important.

And what about nutmeg? That deliciously spicy nutty flavour we all associate with autumn and Christmas? Ingesting as little as two teaspoons could cause you to hallucinate, have seizures and become extremely drowsy.

Pretty much everyone knows you have to soak raw kidney beans and then cook them before you eat them, but not everyone knows why? Raw kidney beans contain lectin, which can cause extremely unpleasant side effects. (You wouldn't be leaving the safety of your toilet for very long, that's for sure!) The process of soaking and boiling the beans removes any danger.

There are more: green potatoes, rhubarb leaves, mushrooms, but I won't continue to bore you. I bet you're shocked at how close you can come to being poisoned on a daily basis though. And think about how trusting you are now you know all of this. How every time someone cooks, or prepares a snack for you, they could quite easily make you seriously unwell or, if they chose, kill you.

My reason for telling you all of this is so you understand how *easy* it is to poison someone with something seemingly innocuous. You really only have to brush past them, drop something into their bag, distract them for a moment. Then you're gone, like a ghost they were barely even aware of.

CHAPTER FIFTEEN

AARON

Aaron's vision blurred and the scene before him swirled. The noise of the engines rushed up to meet his ears and it felt like his senses were in overdrive – it was all too much. He grabbed hold of the bar to steady himself and blinked a few times.

'Poisoned?' he whispered, staring into space.

After a few moments, he gathered himself and addressed the nurse. 'What makes you think she was poisoned?' His voice was a little stronger.

'I believe the white lines on her nails are what is known as Mees' lines, they can indicate heavy metal poisoning. When you add that to the hair loss and her stomach problems, it starts to add up. Did she ever complain of any other pains, or symptoms?'

Aaron shook his head. 'Lydia wasn't a complainer, although, weirdly, she would sometimes get pins and needles for no apparent reason.'

'That would make sense. I'm not an expert, so I can't tell you what she was poisoned with, but if she's been having these symptoms for a while then she was probably being given

frequent small doses, and then potentially a larger, fatal dose.'
Melissa offered Aaron an apologetic look.

'You mean someone has been doing this deliberately?' That
thought hadn't even crossed his mind. 'When you said she'd
been poisoned I assumed it was an accident.'

'I suppose it could be, but I think it unlikely given what we
know.'

Aaron leaned back heavily against the bar and pressed his
fingertips into his eyes. How could this be happening? His
mother dies on board, apparently from a heart attack, and then
Lydia dies a couple of hours later. Was this his payback? Did he
deserve this? Was he really such an awful person?

It was true he did not always see eye to eye with his mother,
he certainly would not have chosen her as a friend, but her loss
did cause him great sadness. He felt a brief moment of guilt as
he remembered his thoughts about Lydia; his wondering if they
loved each other. Their argument before her death brought it
home to him just how badly she had wanted to get married.
How important it was to her, but even now there was the
nagging doubt the *wedding* was the important bit, not the
marriage.

He wouldn't have to wonder about his feelings for Lydia any
longer, nor his motives for proposing any further. The relief he
felt was quickly replaced by shame. How could he possibly be
grateful someone he cared for was dead?

His thoughts tumbled over themselves until one stalled,
stopping front and centre in his mind. 'What about Mother?'

Aaron looked up to see Charley and Melissa chatting
quietly to one another, giving him the space to process what he
had been told. Their eyes flitted from him to one another.

'You mean, do I think she was poisoned?'

'Yes.' The word came out strangled.

Melissa shrugged. 'I don't know. I couldn't see any obvious

signs of poisoning on your mother's body, but I also wasn't looking for them. What makes you think she may have been poisoned?'

'Nothing particularly.' Aaron cast around as if the answer may appear before him. He sighed. 'Maybe I'm just clutching at straws, I don't know.'

'Didn't Lydia say she saw your mother taking some kind of medication just before she passed?' asked Charley.

Aaron nodded. 'She did. She said she thought it was an overdose, but Mother took those awful things all the time. It was nothing unusual. I bet she was immune to them by now. If you look in her suitcase you'll find boxes of them. I'm certain she was addicted, she denied it of course.'

'*If* she was poisoned, it wasn't with the same thing as Lydia – your mother has none of the symptoms Lydia does.'

'Oh, I don't know. I can't think straight.'

Aaron felt a warm hand on his arm and looked up to see Melissa's dark brown eyes watching him.

'If you would like, I can examine your mother's body as well? See if I can put your mind at rest?'

This was oddly one of the kindest things anyone had offered to do for him and the tears welled in his eyes and began to flow freely down his cheeks.

'Thank you,' he breathed, 'that's very kind of you.'

'I can't promise anything, there may be nothing to find,' warned Melissa, 'but I can at least take a look.'

'I understand.' Aaron pulled himself together; he wiped his tears and tucked in his shirt – a guaranteed way to tell if he was anxious. After setting his shoulders and taking a deep breath, he led the two women back into the cabin and towards his mother's seat.

He stood just beyond his mother and gestured towards where she lay, covered with an aeroplane blanket. 'Please...'

'What's going on?' demanded Rex.

'Melissa is going to take a look at Mother and try to establish if she really did die of natural causes, or if she was poisoned like Lydia,' Aaron whispered to his father. Saying it any louder would make it feel real and he didn't want that until he knew for sure.

'Over my dead body!' Rex seemed to fail to understand the irony of his words.

'Father, please, stop creating a scene.'

'I'll do whatever I like and there's no one here to create a *scene* in front of anyway. I will not have some... some stranger defiling my wife's body!' Back was the Glaswegian accent and the bare-faced aggression.

'Mr Fortescue, I am going to have to remind you of our agreement from earlier. Please calm down. Perhaps you would prefer to wait in the bar?' said Charley.

Aaron nodded at Charley, grateful for her timely intervention.

'Dad, I think Charley's right, perhaps you should go and wait in the bar, maybe have a whisky and see how Lydia's parents are doing?' Aaron had noticed the Grant-Fernsbys leave their seats as soon as Charley had made her suggestion.

Rex didn't look like he was going anywhere fast, but he also seemed to realise he was walking a tightrope with the cabin crew.

Melissa offered her own placation. 'Mr Fortescue, I promise I'll be gentle and I *will* retain your wife's dignity at all times.'

'I don't suppose you've left me with much choice.'

'It'll be okay, Dad. I'll be through in a minute.' Aaron gave Rex a gentle nudge towards the bar.

The three watched as Rex parted the curtain into the bar and their shoulders lowered by several inches.

'Should I...' Melissa gestured towards the dead woman.

'Please,' replied Aaron.

He watched as Melissa gently removed the blanket and was surprised to see that his mother didn't look very different. It was only when Melissa started to examine her body that he realised she was having difficulty moving her limbs and rigor mortis must have started to set in.

He watched as Melissa softly checked his mother's nails, arms and eyes. She probed her head carefully and used the torch on her phone to try to see into her mouth.

After a few minutes, Melissa had completed her brief examination and put the blanket back over Vivian's body, ensuring she was as covered as possible.

'There's nothing here that I can see which would point to poison, but that doesn't necessarily mean that she *wasn't* poisoned. There are enough toxins out there that wouldn't show any outward signs. I think we'll have to wait for the post-mortem, I'm sorry.'

Aaron hung his head and was still for a few moments. 'It's okay. Thank you for trying, I really do appreciate it.'

'Oh, sorry! I didn't mean to intrude.'

They all turned to see one of the cabin crew from economy had burst through the curtains separating the cabins.

'It's okay, Hannah, did you need something?' asked Charley.

'I just needed to get some of the snack packs, but it's okay I can come back later.' She was looking around the cabin and appeared to be noting the absence of passengers.

'No, that's all right, you're here now, you might as well get them.'

Hannah moved to the other aisle so she didn't have to squeeze past them and as she did so, she turned and screwed up her nose. 'What's that smell?'

'What smell?' asked Melissa, her interest piqued.

'I'm not sure, but it's a bit odd. I can't put my finger on it. Can none of you smell it?'

Aaron shook his head and saw the others do the same, only Melissa looked like she was deep in thought.

The flight attendant shrugged and carried on, in a hurry to complete her task. Who could blame her? Who would want to be around two corpses for any longer than absolutely necessary?

'I'd better go and check my father's behaving. Charley, I can't tell you how sorry I am again for his behaviour.'

Charley watched as her colleague left the cabin. 'Please don't worry, I fully appreciate these are extremely stressful times for him, for all of you.'

'Yes, but it's also extremely stressful for you to have two passengers die on board, and I wish he would remember that.'

Charley smiled tightly in reply. 'Can I ask you a question?'

'Of course,' replied Aaron unsure what was coming.

'Your father's accent, well... it seems to... change when he's angry or emotional.'

It was Aaron's turn to smile. 'Yes, he's originally from Glasgow and the accent you hear when he's upset is his natural one. When he and my mother got married, it was because she was pregnant with me, and my grandparents insisted on it. However, as you can probably tell, my family can be quite... snobby, I suppose is the right word, and insisted he learn to speak as we do. They taught him our version of manners and turned him into what they considered to be a respectable young man. But underneath all of their meddling, he's still a Glaswegian born and bred and there's nothing wrong with that. To be honest, I rather wish they'd left him alone and let him be himself, but there we go.'

'That certainly explains a few things. And how sad for your father.'

Aaron nodded.

Hannah poking her head through the curtain suddenly. 'I've just realised what that smell is like. Almonds.'

'Almonds?' Melissa whipped her head round to look at the corpse.

'Yeah, it's really weird none of you can smell it.'

'Perhaps not as weird as you might think,' replied Melissa softly.

Hannah shrugged in a noncommittal sort of way and disappeared back to where she came from.

'What are you thinking?' asked Aaron.

'I'm not one hundred per cent certain. I really need to check on a few things. Charley, is there any way at all for me to get internet access up here?'

Charley was watching Melissa with curiosity. 'Yeah, it can be arranged. Let me sort something out.'

'Thanks,' replied the young woman, still lost in her thoughts. 'I need to get back to Theo, you know where I'll be.'

'Sure.'

'Melissa,' called Aaron as she turned to leave, 'thank you – for everything. You've been so kind.'

She waved off his thanks and returned to cattle class.

CHAPTER SIXTEEN

MELISSA

Five hours to landing

Melissa arrived back at her seat to find Theo happily being read to by an older woman with greying curly hair, who clearly remembered a time when people dressed up to travel. It was the same woman who had spoken to them in the departure lounge before the flight.

The woman looked up with gentle green eyes as Melissa approached and smiled. 'I hope you don't mind, the flight attendant needed to help someone who was being a pain and I offered to take over.'

'Oh, thank you, that was very kind of you.'

'I don't really know what's going on up there, but I figured it must be important since you've been gone a while.'

'You could say that, yes,' replied Melissa with a sardonic smile.

The woman laid her hand gently on Melissa's shoulder. 'Well, you're back now, so let me get out of your way. You look like you could use some rest. Let me know if you need me again. I really don't mind and it's not like I've got anything else to do or anywhere else to be.'

Melissa wasn't quite sure where the tears came from; tiredness, stress or this stranger's unconditional kindness, but they started to flow freely and she couldn't stop them.

The woman pulled Melissa into a grandmotherly hug. 'Oh, now now, dear, come here.'

Melissa realised in that moment it had been so long since someone had hugged her, since someone had even touched her with kindness. Theo gave her several hugs a day and she appreciated every single one of them, but it wasn't the same as adult contact.

'Mama?'

She heard Theo's voice from behind her and stepped out of the woman's grasp. His eyes were also filling with tears, not used to seeing his mother so upset.

'It's okay, baby. Mama's okay.' Melissa wiped the tears from her face.

She bent down and picked him up, squeezing him in a great big cuddle. 'Tighter, tighter, tighter,' she said in his ear and he giggled. It was a game they'd played since Theo was old enough to understand and it never failed to make him laugh and try to squeeze Melissa as tightly as he could in return.

Theo looked very serious. 'Shall we have a snack now?'

'Yes, I think we should.'

The woman patted Melissa lightly on the back. 'I'll leave you two to it.'

'Thank you again. What's your name, by the way? I'm Melissa and this is Theo.'

'Margaret, but you can call me Maggie, almost everyone does.'

'Thanks for your help, Maggie.'

Melissa settled Theo in his seat while she opened the overhead locker and, putting one foot on the seat to boost herself up, retrieved her rucksack.

A few minutes later, Theo was happily snacking on a cheese string and some crisps, with a Fruit Shoot to wash it all down with.

While she waited for her promised internet access, she entertained Theo by drawing different shapes and asking him to name them. She couldn't help but marvel at how unaffected he was. Of course he had no idea there were two dead bodies on board the aeroplane, but Melissa had not been by his side for a large chunk of the flight.

It seemed he was happy in other people's company and she supposed she should be grateful for that, at least he wasn't a clingy child. He would likely be quite happy in Barbados as long as there was someone to give him attention. That was certainly her hope, but she still felt a little sadness that he didn't need her as much as she wanted him to.

It didn't take long for Charley to provide her with some wifi log-on details which meant Melissa wouldn't have to pay for the privilege. After checking Theo was quite happy with his colouring book, she pulled out a notebook and pen, and started googling in earnest.

She tackled Lydia's death first, since Melissa was almost certain she had been poisoned. After listing her symptoms, both those she had seen for herself and those which Aaron had mentioned, Google returned a few million hits. Melissa read the first two articles in their entirety and then skimmed through the next half dozen or so since they seemed to confirm what the first two had suggested.

Although it would need a post-mortem to be certain, Melissa was pretty sure Lydia had been poisoned with thallium. Most probably in small doses to begin with, since the symptoms had been around for a while, and then with one final massive dose, the understanding of which brought about a whole new host of questions. Although, if the murderer had continued to spike her food and drink with small doses, in all likelihood she would have died eventually anyway.

What was most disturbing was that thallium was difficult to get hold of in the UK. The articles she read all said it used to be found in rat poison and pesticides, but those had been made illegal years earlier for this very reason – people would use it to poison someone. This all meant whoever poisoned Lydia Grant-Fernsby would have had to order the thallium from somewhere. Although, Melissa supposed, this might actually make the murderer easier to find since there would be a trail and there were only so many people on board who could have administered the fatal dose. Unless Lydia had inadvertently brought the poison on board with her?

After making some notes so Charley could pass the information on to Aaron Fortescue, Melissa began the difficult task of trying to figure out if Vivian Fortescue had also been poisoned and therefore murdered. The one clue she did have though, was the almond smell Hannah had reported, and also the fact she was the only person to mention it.

This time Melissa spent the best part of an hour reading articles and disappearing down rabbit holes to try to confirm her suspicions. She refined her search terms a dozen or more times, before she concluded it was possible that Vivian had been poisoned with cyanide. The smell of almonds all but confirmed it. And the reason only Hannah could smell it was quite simple according to the research Melissa had read; only around 20% of adults could smell cyanide, exactly like bitter almonds.

She was tempted to rush off and tell Charley and the families of the deceased women what she had discovered, but made herself sit and mull it over for a few minutes. What good would she be doing by telling them what she had found? It was supposition after all.

Or was it? Lydia had definitely been poisoned, which meant there was an excellent chance there was a murderer on board. It couldn't have been accidental, because thallium was virtually impossible to find anywhere – it had to be ordered specifically.

The more Melissa turned it over in her mind, the more she understood that in reality, she had, at the very least, a moral obligation to inform the cabin crew what was going on. Someone had killed at least one person, possibly two, and who knew who else might be at risk. She looked down at Theo and with a jolt realised how glad she was she'd brought his snacks with her. It wasn't up to her to decide who was given that information, there were potentially more lives at stake. She had to tell Charley.

Melissa pressed her call button and waited for someone to answer, and a few moments later, she and Charley were talking in hushed tones in the galley at the back of the plane. Maggie had again offered to entertain Theo, saying she was more than happy to do so. Melissa had felt a tug that meant she wanted him close by, but at the same time, she didn't want to have this discussion in front of her son. Reasoning she wouldn't be more than a few minutes and she would be able to see Theo from where she stood, she agreed.

Melissa explained everything she had found out, and all that she surmised, to Charley.

'So, it's possible that someone on this plane has murdered two people, but I can say with some certainty, they have definitely killed one person. It also started before they got on the plane, Lydia Grant-Fernsby has been inadvertently taking thallium for at least a couple of weeks I would think.'

Melissa watched as Charley's face paled and Melissa tried to give the woman some positive news.

'*But*, it looks like they are only targeting the wedding party, I don't think any of the other passengers are at risk.'

'But we can't know that for certain.' Charley was horrified.

'No, that's true, but we can presume that to be the case based on what we do know.'

Charley looked thoughtful for a moment. 'So, you think the fatal dose of thallium had to be given on the plane?'

'I think it had to be. Lydia would have died quite quickly after ingesting it. If she'd taken it before we took off, I think she would have died much earlier in the flight.'

'So, does that mean it's someone in first class? Since, other than you, no one else has been in there.'

'Well, me and the flight attendants of course. But actually, it doesn't even mean whoever was giving her the poison is on board. They could have dropped something into her bag knowing she would eat or drink it.'

'Oh God, it gets worse,' replied Charley as the obvious occurred to her. 'It can't be a member of cabin crew, it just can't be.'

'Probably not. Don't forget someone has been poisoning Lydia for a couple of weeks, so it's much more likely it's someone she knows.'

'Someone from the wedding party, you mean?'

'Exactly.'

Charley slumped back, her head in her hands. She stayed that way for over a minute before she looked up, apparently having come to a decision. 'Right, what we need–'

Melissa raised her hands. '*We?* I'm sorry, but I'm not getting any more involved than I already am. I know I said it was unlikely whoever killed Lydia would kill other passengers, but if they think I'm involved, or they think I might know who they are, that makes me a target. And I have to think of Theo; if something happens to me, who will look after him? No – I'm staying out of it from now on.'

'Please, Melissa. You're a nurse.'

'That's right, a nurse, not a detective, or a doctor or anything that means I need to be involved. I can't do anything more for those two dead women, but I can protect me and my son. You have all of the information – you know as much as I do.'

Charley's shoulders dropped in defeat. 'You're right, I'm sorry, I shouldn't have even asked.'

'It's okay, I understand why you did. Here, take my notes and just tell them what I told you. It might be worth checking to see if there is a policeman on board.'

'I checked before and there isn't. Thank you for this. I'll need to let the captain know what's going on too. All of this would have to happen on a flight with no air protection officer on board, wouldn't it?'

Melissa returned to her seat, thanking Maggie once more for minding Theo, hopefully for the last time. Melissa made sure her son was happy and tuned in to a movie. She was determined this would be the start of her holiday proper and she would have no more to do with that crazy family in first class.

CHAPTER SEVENTEEN

CHARLEY

Four and a half hours to landing

Not for the first time, Charley wished there were more places to hide on an aeroplane. She needed a place away from prying eyes and constant requests so she could stop and think about everything that had occurred in the last three or four hours. God! Was this flight really only four hours in? It felt like she'd been on board for a week. More had happened on this flight already than had happened on most of her other flights put together, and she had a horrible feeling there was more to come.

She was acutely aware the rest of her colleagues were doing a miraculous job holding down the fort. She also knew the passengers not involved in the *situation*, as she now thought of it, would be asking all sorts of difficult questions of her co-workers and she was grateful to them for not bothering her and doing their best to answer. She owed them – big time – and as soon as she had a spare moment she would gather them together and tell them that.

For now though, she spied a vacant toilet and slid inside, locking the door behind her. As the light came on, she looked in the large mirror in front of her and gave herself a talking to.

'You just need to tell Liz what's going on and go from there. She'll advise you what to do next. This is not your fault, this is not your doing – you're just doing your job, and you're bloody good at it.'

Charley lowered the seat lid on the toilet and sat. She read through Melissa's notes a couple of times and made some of her own to jog her memory. After a while she realised she couldn't put it off anymore. Or rather, she could, but it wouldn't be of any benefit to anyone. Least of all herself.

She'd never spoken to a captain so often on a flight – even a long-haul one. This would be one of the famous journeys, talked about for years and passed on to new recruits as one of *those* stories.

'Hi Liz, it's Charley.'

'Hey, how's it going out there?'

'Not great, to be honest. I need to fill you in on some stuff.'

'Okay, you have my attention.'

'Another person has died, this time it's Lydia, the bride.' Charley paused to allow Liz to absorb the information.

'What the fuck?'

'I know, but there's more, we think she was poisoned. And it might have been going on for a while.'

There was an audible gasp on the other end of the intercom. *'Are you sure?'*

'As sure as we can be.'

'We?'

'There's a nurse on board who's been helping me, she's done some research and it all adds up.'

98

'*Right, you better fill me in.*'

'Okay.' Charley picked up the notebook and skimmed the notes to prompt her. She realised her hand was shaking; telling someone else this information made it all seem a bit too real. Could there really be a killer on board their plane? 'Obviously, this will all need to be confirmed by the police when we get there, but–'

'*I get that, just tell me what you're thinking.*'

'Melissa, she's the nurse, she suspected straight away that Lydia had been poisoned. There were some signs on the woman's body that made her suspicious. After doing some research, she is reasonably sure Lydia has been poisoned with thallium. It's a colourless, odourless, tasteless heavy metal – it used to be found in rat poison and the like.'

'*Rat poison?*'

'Yeah, but here's the thing, it's really hard to get hold of in the UK these days. Someone would have had to special order it, so this isn't a mistake. She's been unwell for a few weeks, which means this has been going on for some time and the symptoms she had been experiencing were something to do with that.'

'*Right…*' Liz drew the word out, as if she knew there was more to come.

'Given the research Melissa has read about thallium and the way it works in the body, it looks like the final fatal dose was administered here on the aeroplane.'

'*Are you telling me there's a killer on board my aircraft?*'

'I'm saying there might be, but it's also possible Lydia ate or drank it via something she brought on board in her bag.'

'*Isn't that just wonderful! Anything else you need to tell me?*'

'There is a thought that perhaps Vivian Fortescue was also poisoned.'

'*What?*' Charley winced as Liz shouted in her ear. '*I thought the old bag died of a heart attack?*'

'We thought the same, or at least we had no reason to suspect otherwise until Hannah walked past.'

'Hannah? What's Hannah got to do with anything?'

Charley realised she wasn't making much sense and decided to get straight to the point. 'When she walked past, she said she could smell almonds, but she was the only person who could smell it. When Melissa was online she looked it up and it turns out cyanide smells like bitter almonds, but not everyone can actually smell it apparently.'

'Cyanide? Are you fucking serious? How the fuck does someone get cyanide on board an aircraft?'

'We think it was in her medication. Apparently she takes these powdered painkillers like they're going out of fashion and Lydia saw her take one right before she died. We had thought it might be an overdose since she was also seen necking one before she got on board, but the whole smelling of almonds thing changed that.'

Charley stopped speaking and waited for Liz to say something. She imagined the woman staring at her handset, not quite believing the words coming out of the earpiece.

'Liz?'

'Just give me a second, I need to think.'

'Sure.'

Despite everything, Charley felt a sense of relief that she was sharing the problem with someone else; someone who wasn't a civilian. Liz was just as responsible as she was and they could shoulder the burden together.

'From what you've told me, there's a good chance there's someone on board who's killing people. And I think, from a passenger safety point of view, we have to assume that is the case. Since we don't know for sure how these poisons got on board, we have to assume they could be anywhere, including in our

supplies. *Therefore, from now on, we are suspending food and drink service.'*

'We still have half the flight to go though. People will be hungry and thirsty, and some of them are already questioning what's going on.'

'I get that, but I'm sure they'll understand when they find out our concern was to get them to Barbados alive.'

'True.' Charley chewed at her lip trying to think of a solution. 'What if we only hand out sealed items? Everyone has already had their meal anyway, so we can be sure that isn't contaminated, otherwise we'd have bodies everywhere. We just won't give out ice, or fruit juice, or things like that.'

'That could work. Okay, let's go with that. But keep me updated, and the slightest sign someone is unwell, we shut it all down. In the meantime, I'll report the second death to ground control.'

'Agreed.'

'What about the family?'

'They know Melissa was going to check online for information, so they'll ask me even if I don't offer it. I don't see any reason to keep it from them.'

'Okay. Let me know how it goes when you get the chance. Good luck.'

'Thanks, I'm going to need it.'

Charley replaced the handset and before she could think any more about it, she walked quickly towards the stairs.

Where once the beautiful lighting and opulent decor had made her feel lucky to work in such a place, now it made her think of walking into the lions' den.

CHAPTER EIGHTEEN

AARON

Aaron heard the footsteps coming up the stairs and turned round, standing to watch whoever it was. He had assumed it would be Melissa coming to tell them all what she had found, so was surprised when Charley appeared.

'Has Melissa discovered anything yet?'

Charley smiled politely and walked toward the front of the cabin where everyone could see her. 'She has given me some information that she has asked me to pass on to you.'

'Wait, where's Melissa?' asked Aaron. 'I thought she might be here.'

'She has a small son on board with her and needs to take care of him.'

Aaron nodded. 'Of course.'

He looked around at his remaining fellow passengers. The Grant-Fernsbys were holding hands, their red-rimmed eyes eager for information. Rex was on his feet, his whole body tense, and Darius was leaning forward in his seat, ready to receive whatever Charley had to transmit.

'Why don't you all take a seat?'

They did as they were bid, only Rex remained standing.

Charley looked to him in expectation. 'Mr Fortescue?'

'Dad, sit down.'

'I want to know what's going on, son,' he said, but without taking his eyes from Charley.

'We all do, and Charley's about to tell us.'

Rex remained standing for what Aaron thought was a bit too long.

'Dad, sit down.' This time Aaron tugged his father by the arm.

Finally Rex did as he was bid and took a seat, all the while staring at Charley.

After a moment or two, she took a deep breath and started speaking.

Aaron listened as Charley relayed everything she had been told by Melissa and the conclusions that had been drawn. There were words he'd heard, but the context seemed so incongruous that he struggled to wrap his mind around what he was hearing.

Poison.

Thallium.

Killer.

On board.

Archibald stood suddenly. 'Do you mean to say you suspect the person who murdered our daughter might be here on this very aircraft?'

He had gone rather red in the face and looked like he might explode at any second. Gone was the softly spoken giant, and before her stood a grizzly bear ready to defend its family.

'Oh dear.' Daphne's words might have been the biggest understatement Aaron had ever heard.

'And what about Mother?'

'You might remember that Hannah, one of the cabin crew, mentioned she could smell almonds when she walked past?' Aaron nodded his agreement. 'That sparked something in

Melissa's mind and when she was researching she included that in her search terms.'

'Included *what* in her search terms?'

'The fact that only one person could smell it.'

'Cyanide,' whispered Darius.

No one hid their surprise as he uttered the word.

'Yes, but how could you possibly know that?'

Cyanide? What...?

'But how would you poison someone with cyanide? And on an aeroplane of all places?'

'It's easy.' Darius shrugged, looking utterly miserable. 'It's found in all sorts of fruit pips. Grind them up and sprinkle them on food...'

'Or onto a powder you know that person is going to take really soon,' whispered Aaron. 'She took those painkillers all the time, everyone knew it, and she took one right before she died.'

Rex broke his silence. 'Does that mean we're *all* targets now?'

'I really don't know, but it does appear there might be a murderer on board and they know their poisons,' said Charley.

Rex got to his feet. 'It's obvious then, isn't it? It has to be Darius.'

Aaron stood quickly and manoeuvred himself between his father and his best friend, towering over his father.

'Don't be ridiculous, Dad, Darius isn't a killer. Why would he want to kill Mother and Lydia? It's a completely ludicrous accusation, just because he happened to know a couple of facts anyone could have learned from the internet?'

'I'll tell you why he did it,' snarled Rex.

Despite his dark skin, Darius's face paled, his expression panicked. Whatever it was Rex knew, Darius did not want everyone else to know.

'Please... don't...'

'He did it because he's in love with you and he wants you for himself. He knew your mother would never accept it if you were gay, and he needed to get Lydia out of the way too.'

It was as if someone had flicked a switch on a vacuum and all the air was sucked from the room. The noise of the engine roared in Aaron's ears and the cabin walls felt like they were closing in on him. It was...

'Don't be so ridiculous, Dad.' Aaron was looking between his father and Darius. It couldn't be true, could it?

'It's not ridiculous. Tell him, Darius, tell him what you did.'

Aaron focused on Darius, willing him to answer, but he saw the look on his best man's face and decided to bail him out.

'Whatever he did isn't important, Darius knows I'm not gay. There's no way he would ever think I might be in love with him, and I seriously doubt he's in love with me.'

'Fine, if he won't tell you, then I will. When he was staying at our house last year I walked in on him and he was, well, he was giving himself a good time.' Rex had clearly altered his word choices in deference to the company.

'Whilst that's a pretty embarrassing situation, it means nothing here and now.'

'He was watching a video of you, son.'

As Rex said the words, Darius dropped his head to his hands and groaned.

The only sound was of the engines roaring. No one said a word; shocked faces watched Aaron who swayed as he reached for support.

'Is it true?'

Without removing his hands from his face, Darius simply nodded.

Aaron looked at him for a few seconds before making a decision.

'Darius, let's go to the bar. I think we need to talk.'

CHAPTER NINETEEN

People often say they are prepared to do anything for their loved ones. They say they'd *die* for someone they love, or they'd *kill* for someone they love. I've always wondered if that were true. If you were called upon to die for a person you love, by, say, jumping in front of a gunman, or killing yourself so they could have your heart, would you do it?

What if someone badly hurt, killed or raped a person you loved? Could you really go after the culprit and kill them for it?

I know people kill in the name of love, we read it in the papers often enough, but is that the start? Or are we only hearing about them because they are so unusual? Or are these people really just the jealous kind and claiming they killed in the name of love? I find it's usually the latter, and in actual fact they're killing in the name of control and manipulation.

I think it far more likely someone would kill rather than *die* for a person they loved. But then, maybe I'm just cynical.

What I can tell you is that I have killed in the name of love and I would be prepared to do so again. Because, dear reader, that is exactly what I'm doing now, here on this aeroplane. I'm killing for someone I love and I just hope they appreciate it. I truly would do anything for them and, even if I do get caught, I am more than prepared to go to prison for my crimes.

And I would be sent to prison if I were caught because poisoning someone is such a deliberate act. Poisoning requires planning and preparation and it would be virtually impossible to claim you had poisoned someone 'by accident'. All that organisation and groundwork couldn't be considered as anything other than 'premeditated'. Ipso facto – you're a murderer. Go directly to jail, do not pass go, do not collect £200.

Having said that though, and you can call me arrogant if you like, I seriously doubt if even Poirot himself could catch me. I have read enough books, both fiction and non-fiction, to know how to cover my tracks, as they say. And this is one of those curious things about modern culture – everyone is so desperate to read a 'how to' guide that authors are falling over themselves to write them. The true crime lovers out there are worshipped for their voracious appetites by people like me. People who want to get away with their actions and hide their crimes.

When you add to that just how much information is available on the internet – being careful to clear down your history correctly and naturally – then it's really a surprise anyone is caught doing anything these days. There are, of course, the spectacularly stupid out there, there is nothing to be done about them. Although, giving it some thought, perhaps it's a good thing these dumb criminals are still being caught. It means the police look for easy wins and are less likely to come after the more trying cases on their desks.

I digress, where was I? Ah yes, doing anything in the name of love. I can only hope my actions lead to the greatest love in my life being able to lead the life they want to. To be free of judgement and ridicule, and to be the happiest they can possibly be. Isn't that all any of us wishes for our friends and family? To be happy and content? The only difference here is that I am willing to do something about it. I am willing to take that very large step to make sure it happens.

In case you were wondering – I am very willing to kill for my love, but I would rather not die if it can be at all avoided.

CHAPTER TWENTY

AARON

Darius sat hard on the plush bench in the first class bar as soon as he entered the room. His head hung low and his hands gripped the back of his neck, his fingers intertwined. Aaron could feel the humiliation coming off him and his heart went out to his friend, it really did.

That didn't mean his thoughts and feelings weren't confused though. Of course he felt sorry for him being shamed and embarrassed by Rex, but he couldn't wrap his head around the fact his best friend, a man he'd known for years, was in *love* with him? Seriously?

They'd gone to university together, lived together after first year, and of course Aaron knew he was gay, it wasn't something Darius had ever hidden. But this? This was a whole new level of, well, *weird*. No, not weird exactly, but odd – a bit uncomfortable. Aaron didn't know what to think. Actually, a lot more uncomfortable since he found out Darius had masturbated over him. He didn't want to look at that too closely though, there was enough going on.

Even though Charley had told him they were not going to be serving anything that wasn't sealed, Aaron went behind the bar and poured them both a drink: brandy for him, whisky for Darius. He remembered their conversation earlier about not getting drunk on spirits – it seemed like a lifetime ago, but actually couldn't have been more than an hour or two. He grimaced, too much had happened on this flight already and he wasn't prepared to face any more of it without at least another brandy inside of him. And he definitely wouldn't blame Darius for wanting to get absolutely smashed now.

Aaron nudged Darius and handed him his tumbler of whisky. He moved and sat on the other end of the bench. He wanted to create a bit of space between them – they both needed it. Aaron had no idea what he should say, how does anyone even react to that kind of revelation? He took a long sip of his drink and tried to think of a way to start the conversation. The brandy was a nice drop, but it burned in Aaron's stomach as it mixed with the adrenaline caused by his father's announcement.

'Darius, mate, I–'

Darius cut him off without looking up. 'You don't have to say anything. I don't blame you for hating me.'

This was not what Aaron had been expecting. Did he hate Darius? He took a moment. 'I don't hate you, why would you think that?'

'Because I've embarrassed you in front of everyone.'

'No, my father embarrassed *you* in front of everyone. And trust me, I will be having words with him.' Aaron's initial awkwardness was now replaced by annoyance towards his father.

'You don't need to do that, what he said was true.'

'That doesn't give him the right to tell everyone something you clearly didn't want them to know. And for what it's worth, I totally understand why you kept it a secret. It must have been... difficult for you.'

'Please don't give me any sympathy, I can't stand it.'

Aaron fumbled for the right words, but everything that came into his head didn't sound quite right. As he tried to form a sentence that didn't sound contrived, a different thought came to him. 'My father didn't hold this over you, did he? Did he threaten to tell people? To tell me?'

'Not specifically, but he didn't need to. Whenever I was around he'd give me this look, like he found me disgusting. I know what he thinks of me, what he thinks of people like me and when he caught me, well... it didn't help, did it?'

The two men lapsed into silence. Aaron knew he needed to say something, to be clear. He allowed a few minutes to pass before he spoke again.

'Look, I... I don't know if I need to say this or not, but I'm going to say it anyway, for the avoidance of doubt just in case.' Aaron winced at how formal he sounded. 'You know I don't... you know I'm not gay, right? You know there won't ever be an "us" in the roma–?'

'Of course I know that!' Darius interrupted. 'You don't have to spell it out for me, I'm not an idiot.'

'I don't think you are. I just... well, I just thought it best to be clear, that's all.' Aaron hoped his words came across as compassionately as possible, whilst still having an air of finality about them.

'You've been *very* clear. I knew it would never happen, but I did think we would always be mates and that would be enough. Not going to happen now though, is it?' The bitterness and sadness dripped from every word Darius spoke.

'What? Why wouldn't we be mates anymore?'

When Darius didn't reply, Aaron continued, 'We've been friends for *years*, why would I give that up now? I should be flattered really. Are things a bit weird? Yeah, but we'll get over that. Besides, you have to be my friend, you know *way* too many of my secrets.'

The last comment raised a half smile from Darius. Aaron moved closer, clapping a hand on his friend's shoulders and giving it a squeeze. 'If you accept nothing is ever going to happen and we will only ever be friends, then I still want you around.'

'But what about the other thing your dad said? About me being the one who killed your mum and Lydia?'

Darius's questions caused Aaron to pause and reflect. His father's accusations and rationale certainly made sense – people have killed for less – but could Darius really be capable of murder? Could he really kill two people in order to get to a man he says he knew would never be his? Did Darius think he might be able to persuade Aaron, in his grief, to be with him?

Aaron just couldn't see it. He'd known his best friend for over twenty years, and nothing in all that time had given him pause for thought. Darius didn't even get into fights, he was a peacemaker; usually the one to stop fights before they flared up and became physical. And *poison*, wasn't that traditionally a woman thing? He seemed to remember reading or hearing that somewhere, probably on one of the True Crime podcasts he liked to listen to.

The thought of poison brought images of test tubes and bunsen burners to mind, and a man with check shirt and bow tie wearing a white lab coat. He chuckled to himself until he remembered chemistry had been Darius's favourite subject at school – he'd been awarded an A*. Could you make poisons in a chemistry lab? Did it follow that if you're good at chemistry you would know about, or how to make, poisons?

Aaron let out a low groan, his thoughts swirling around in his head. He scrubbed at his face and looked up to see Darius staring at him with a slightly incredulous look on his face.

'Well? Do you or do you not believe I had something to do with their deaths?'

Aaron thought for a moment longer and realised deep down, in his heart of hearts, he did not believe the man sitting before him was capable of murder – for any reason.

'No, I don't think you did. I just don't know *who* though. I mean who could possibly be a suspect?'

CHAPTER TWENTY-ONE

MELISSA

After Melissa handed over the information she had gathered to Charley, refusing to take any further part in the drama in first class, she had returned to her seat to watch a film. She was determined she would have nothing more to do with any of them, but that didn't stop her mind from being curious, or her wondering if she'd done the right thing.

After a few minutes she decided to put it firmly out of her mind and concentrate on the film in front of her. She'd started to watch *Pretty Woman* earlier, but after the interruption she didn't feel much like going back to it. Instead she decided on good old Harry Potter for a bit of escapism; something to take her mind off everything that had happened in the few hours she'd been on board.

A short while later, whilst fully engrossed in *The Order of the Phoenix* (which turned out to be a better film than the book would have suggested), she caught sight of Charley. She was moving up the other aisle her face a contortion of stress and misery. Melissa returned to her film and tried to tune back in but to no avail.

Her mind kept going over what might have happened and

how the two families had reacted. She gave her head a shake and tried to concentrate while Harry shouted at his friends for not writing him letters over the summer.

After a few minutes her mind wandered again, and in an exasperated sigh, she hit pause and pulled out her headphones. She spun round in her seat, craning her neck to look up the aisle behind her to see if she could see Charley anywhere.

Unable to see much, she undid her seat belt and stood. Theo was still happily scribbling away, so she touched Maggie gently on the shoulder and asked the lady to keep an eye on Theo one more time.

'I won't be long, a few minutes. He's quite happy where he is, I just don't want him running off anywhere.'

'Don't you worry, pet, I'll keep an eye on him.'

After thanking the woman, she made her way up the aisle to the galley at the rear of the plane. She wasn't quite sure what she was going to ask, or even if Charley would tell her anything. After all, she had refused to take any further part in the 'drama'. Thinking on it now, to call the death and possible murder of two women 'drama' was probably a bit callous. At least she didn't say it to the family she rationalised.

Melissa found Charley in the galley rummaging in one of the trollies. She jumped when Melissa said her name.

'Sorry, I didn't mean to startle you.'

'It's okay,' replied Charley as she poked her head out the door and checked either side. After she had assured herself Melissa was the only one there, she continued her rummaging and produced a small bottle of gin.

'I really shouldn't be doing this,' she said, unscrewing the bottle top, 'but this has been one helluva flight already.' With that, she swigged back the entire contents of the bottle and gasped.

Melissa must have looked a little shocked because Charley

said, 'Don't worry, I don't make a habit of it and certainly won't be getting pissed. You're still in safe hands.' She produced a tube of Polo mints and popped two in her mouth, then offered some to Melissa who declined.

'Are you okay? What happened up there?'

'I'll be fine. I thought you didn't want to get involved anymore?'

'I don't, but you looked upset and I'm about the only other person, not involved, who knows what's going on, so I thought I'd come and check on you.'

'Sorry.' Charley's shoulders fell and the harsh look on her face was gone. 'It's just all a bit stressful.'

'I bet it is. What happened when you told them? Were they upset?'

'They were upset, yes, but less about the information I gave them and more about Rex's big revelation.'

'What do you mean?'

Charley sighed. 'He accused Darius of being the murderer.'

'Darius? The best friend? But why?'

'Because it turned out Darius is gay and completely in love with Aaron. And Rex knows this because he caught Darius...' Charley paused before lowering her voice to a whisper, '... masturbating over a video of Aaron.'

'Oh my God! You're joking? And Aaron didn't know?'

'Didn't have a clue. I mean, he knows his friend's gay, but definitely not the part about him being in love with him. I've left them to talk it out in the bar. Please don't tell anyone I've told you, I'm being so unprofessional, but I feel like you deserve to know.'

'I won't tell anyone, but what if he *is* the killer though and you've left him alone with Aaron? What if he tries to poison Aaron too?'

'He *loves* Aaron, he's not about to poison him. Besides, Aaron was insistent that they be left alone.'

There wasn't much more to say after that; Melissa visited the bathroom before making her way back to her seat.

When she arrived, Theo had fallen asleep again, his pencil in hand. Melissa gently removed it and manoeuvred him into a more comfortable position, placing his blanket over him.

'I didn't like to move him,' said Maggie. 'I thought he might wake up and I figured you could do with some peace.'

Melissa sat and let out a long slow breath. 'That's okay, you did the right thing.'

'Everything all right, dear?'

With her head still against the head rest, she turned to face the kind lady who had offered up her time so freely and expected nothing in return. She was rewarded with a soft smile and gentle eyes.

'I'm fine, I can't really talk about what's going on.'

'I wouldn't dream of asking you. Now, how about you tell me why you're heading to Barbados all on your lonesome with a toddler in tow. It can't be easy even without all this other... stuff going on.' Maggie waved a hand in the air.

'You're right, it's not easy, but I'm hoping it'll be worth it.'

Melissa waited for Maggie to make a comment, or ask another question, but she just smiled at her.

'I left my ex a little while ago and he's been making life difficult. So I got in contact with an old friend and we made plans to meet in Barbados.'

Maggie winked at her. 'A special friend?'

Melissa felt her cheeks redden and she really didn't know why. 'No, it's nothing like that...' She trailed off unsure what else to say.

'Of course, dear. Whatever it is, it sounds like getting away from an abusive ex is absolutely the right thing to do.'

'Oh, he wasn't abusive.'

'I thought you said he was causing problems? My mistake.'

'He did, but it's not like he hit me or anything. He just... he made life difficult.'

Maggie's face softened. 'Just because he didn't hit you, doesn't mean he didn't abuse you. And if you're having to run away to get him to stop, well, it sounds to me like he was a wrong 'un.'

Melissa smiled at Maggie's vehemence. 'That is true, he certainly was.'

Maggie nodded towards Theo. 'What about the wee one? Will he miss his dad, or is he too young to know the difference?'

Melissa cast her eyes downwards and felt the shame creeping up her neck and onto her face. She knew she'd gone red and she also knew there was nothing she could do about it. Without lifting her eyes, she said, 'He wasn't Theo's dad.'

'If there isn't a silver lining in every cloud. He'll never want to bother looking for him then, will he?'

Melissa looked up, startled by Maggie's response. In her experience, it was usually the older generation who judged her most harshly. If Maggie noticed her reaction, she didn't show it.

'So what about Theo's daddy, does he mind you taking him halfway across the world?'

Melissa hesitated, unsure how to reply, her mouth hanging slightly open.

Maggie's eyes widened a little. 'Don't mind me.' She waved her hand in the air again. 'Too nosey for my own good. My grandkids are always telling me that. It's your business and I've no business asking.'

'No, it's not that.' She hadn't intended to make her feel uncomfortable. 'It's just... complicated. And I don't mind you asking at all.'

Melissa asked the woman about her grandchildren in order

to avoid any more awkward questions and the two women settled into a nice little chat across the aisle.

After a few minutes of back and forth, Maggie yawned loudly and suddenly Melissa could feel her own eyes start to droop.

'Look at the pair of us.' Maggie laughed. 'I think we should both have a nap, make sure we're wide awake for when we arrive.'

Melissa laughed too and in agreement, she pulled her blanket over her and adjusted the pillow behind her head.

A few minutes later she was sleeping soundly.

CHAPTER TWENTY-TWO

CHARLEY

Four hours to landing

Charley was *so* over this flight. She'd been cabin crew for over fifteen years and she absolutely loved her job. She'd done short-haul and long-haul flights in her time, but by and large she much preferred long-haul. In many ways a day of short hops to Scotland or over to the continent were far more exhausting with the constant take-offs and landings, than a straight eight-hour flight to Barbados, or even the long flight from London to Chile, which takes over fourteen hours.

But this flight... this flight had to be the longest and most stressful of her career. She'd experienced demanding passengers before and normally she had all she needed on board to satisfy their every whim – with the possible exception of sea urchins as one first class passenger had requested a few years earlier. One or two demanding customers were to be expected, but to have an entire party of them was exhausting. And then two of them go and die!

Charley knew it was not the fault of the dead women, but she couldn't help but resent the fact they'd died on her flight, when all of the responsibility lay with her. Not to mention the fact there was likely a *murderer* on board. Charley's closeness to all that had happened made everything seem quite normal. She had become desensitised and the realisation made her feel a little sick. She should be shocked, scared, worried, something, but all she wanted was to land and have the Bajan police take over from her.

The Bajan police – shit, she was going to have to make a statement which meant it would be hours even after they landed before she could switch off and treat herself to some local rum punch. At this rate, she'd be forgoing the punch and just mainlining rum.

Charley checked her watch; four hours to go before they landed – over halfway. With a start she realised she hadn't actually eaten anything since long before they'd taken off that morning. No wonder the shot of gin she'd necked earlier was sitting heavy in her tummy. Technically she'd missed her mealtime, but that wasn't her fault and she wouldn't be any use to man nor beast if she fainted while she was carrying out her duties. She opened one of the trollies and found a ham sandwich. After double-checking it was properly sealed, she ate it quickly, washing it down with a bottle of water; ignoring the lure of the miniatures.

'Hey, Charley, is it okay if I take my break now?'

Charley jumped and spun round, one hand clutching at her chest. 'Jesus Christ, you scared the shit out of me.'

Jen winced. 'Sorry. I thought you would've heard me.'

'Don't worry, I was miles away. What was it you said?'

'Can I take my break now? I know it'll have to be a bit shorter than usual, but I'll set an alarm and be up again in time to prepare for landing.'

Charley sighed, technically it was too late for anyone to be taking a break, but it had been an unusual flight and it didn't make sense for everyone to be shattered when they arrived.

'Sure, just two hours though.'

'Thanks, Charley.' Jen peered at her. 'Although, you look like you could use a break yourself. You look knackered.'

Charley tried hard not to roll her eyes. 'Thanks for that. I'll sleep when we get to the hotel.'

Charley watched as the young woman left the galley and for a moment, hankered after the days when she had no responsibility. Back to the days where she could request to take her break and no one would mind. But then, she liked being in charge and more importantly, she liked the extra money that came with the increased responsibility.

With her sandwich finished, it was time to get back to work and check in with her colleagues. After a quick tidy up in the galley, she made her way down the aisle. She appreciated some of the passengers may have questions and she wanted to make herself visible; the rest of her crew had already borne the brunt of their questions for long enough.

Charley had given instructions that the deaths of the two passengers be kept strictly confidential; the last thing they needed was a panic in such an enclosed space.

'Excuse me.'

A nasally voice interrupted her thoughts as she wandered down the aisle. Charley turned round and was faced with a man climbing out of his seat and making his way towards her. His hair was thinning and his face looked like it was permanently screwed up. He was also so short Charley had to stop herself from stooping down to speak to him a bit like she would a small child.

'Yes, sir, how can I help you?'

'You can help me by telling me what's going on up there,' he said loudly, trying to peer around her.

Charley had no idea what he was trying to see, there were only more rows of seats in front of them. 'There's nothing to be concerned about, sir,' she said quietly.

'The constant rushing up and down of your staff seems to suggest otherwise.' He hadn't taken the hint to match her volume.

'Sir, there are people sleeping, perhaps you could lower your voice a touch?'

The man looked like she had just questioned his parentage, rather than asking him to speak more quietly.

'I will speak at whatever volume I please. Now, I demand to know what is going on.'

Charley pulled herself up to her full height and clasped her hands in front of her; she'd had enough.

'Some passengers were taken ill. That is all I can, or will, tell you. I must respect the privacy of all of the passengers on board. You would be extremely angry if I were to tell someone else your personal business, I'm sure.' The man opened his mouth to speak, but Charley wasn't finished. 'Now, if there's nothing else, perhaps you could return to your seat? I would be happy to bring you a beverage if you would like?' Charley's eyes were wide, daring him to question her further.

The man humphed and glared up at her. 'I will be making a complaint about you when we land, what is your name?' He was practically shouting.

'Charley White. Would you like me to spell that for you?' Charley knew she was pushing it, and her voice was no longer calm or level.

'No, that's quite all right, I'm sure I'll manage.' He smirked.

Charley flushed and glanced around, quite a few of the passengers were staring. She smiled at them as best she could, smoothed her hair and then continued walking the rest of the way down the plane.

'Theo?' called a loud voice.

Charley whirled round. She knew that voice and knew that name. She tried to see over the middle seats to where she knew Melissa and Theo were sitting, but she couldn't see either of them.

'Theo?' This time Melissa shouted louder, her voice more panicked.

Charley quickly made her way to Melissa's seat, no mean feat with a full aeroplane.

'Melissa, what's the matter?'

The young woman was on her hands and knees looking under her seat. She twisted her neck to look up at Charley on hearing her name.

'It's Theo, I can't find him.'

CHAPTER TWENTY-THREE

AARON

Aaron looked up as someone poked their head between the curtains.

'I'm sorry to disturb you,' one of the flight attendants said with an apologetic look. Aaron chastised himself for not remembering his name. 'Is it okay if I just grab something from behind the bar?'

Aaron looked at Darius, his head bowed.

Aaron took a deep breath and stood, placing his empty glass on the bar. 'Of course. I'm sorry we've taken so long. Please.'

'Thank you.' The flight attendant moved to behind the bar with light steps.

Aaron placed a hand on his friend's shoulder. 'Where do you want to be, Darius?'

'Anywhere but on this fucking plane.'

Aaron sighed, determined to be patient and not rise to it. 'I get that, but do you want to stay in the bar? Or shall we go back to our seats for a while? It might be easier to relax in your pod.'

'You're right.' Darius's shoulders fell, defeated. 'Let's go.'

Darius hauled himself to his feet, but kept his eyes to the ground. As they passed through the curtains, Aaron pushed them fully open. Darius flopped into his seat and Aaron patted him on the shoulder, continuing to his own seat.

Once seated, Aaron looked around him and saw the Grant-Fernsbys had fallen asleep, Daphne's head on Archibald's shoulder. No doubt they were exhausted after the emotional turmoil they had gone through in the last few hours.

His father caught his eye and Rex was glowering at him. Aaron could not have this conversation with his father, so he averted his eyes, only for it to fall on the covered body of his mother. He was quickly reminded, as if he could have forgotten, that he was also sitting next to two deceased loved ones. The emotion rose in his chest and he tried to swallow it down. It wasn't that he was ashamed to cry, but he felt if he started he might not stop and there was no one else to look after Darius or keep his father in check. Worse than that, he couldn't handle sympathy right now.

He looked at the Grant-Fernsbys and was envious of their peace. Even if it was only for a short time, they were asleep and not thinking about the tragedy which had befallen them all.

Aaron felt utterly drained, his limbs were heavy and he would have liked nothing more than to fall asleep, but he wasn't sure his brain would allow him to. His thoughts were swirling and he couldn't land on and follow once specific train of thought without another jumping in and nudging the first out of the way. That, and he really didn't trust his father to behave.

Aaron dragged his hands down his face and then rubbed at his eyes. He tipped his head back against the rest, his eyes closed, and thought about what to do now. They still had at least a couple of hours before they were due to land and there was quite literally nothing he could do. Watching a film seemed so disrespectful, but he couldn't sit and do nothing. He couldn't just sit and stare straight ahead, wishing the time away, it would drive him mad. Perhaps he could find some music to listen to, something classical without any words.

As he opened his eyes to lean forward, he heard a hissing in his ear.

'So, what did he say?' It was his father.

Trying not to pull a face, Aaron didn't look at Rex, but searched for his headphones in the pocket next to him. 'It's private.'

Rex clamped a hand on his arm and Aaron looked at it pointedly before looking his father in the eye. Rex took the hint and removed his hand, instead crouching so they were at similar heights.

'Did he try to deny it?'

'No, he didn't, but he was utterly mortified. How could you do that to him? How could you expose him like that in front of everyone?'

Rex shrugged. 'He has a motive, I thought people deserved to know.'

'That's ridiculous, Dad. Most of us have motives if you look closely enough, but that doesn't mean it's okay to go around telling people's secrets and embarrassing them like that. You could have waited and mentioned it to the police when we landed.'

'And what if he decides to poison someone else, hey? What then? I was only trying to protect us.'

'Even if that's true, you could have told me privately.'

'Maybe you're right, but it's out in the open now.' Rex had the good grace to look a little embarrassed. 'Was I right, was he the one doing it?'

'God, Dad! No, of course not! Darius never expected us to have a relationship–'

'I should bloody well think not!'

Aaron rolled his eyes. 'Do try to remove yourself from the

dark ages for a moment, Father. Yes, he told me he was in love with me, but he also knew it was never going to happen, whether Lydia and I got married or not. It would be of no advantage to him to kill anyone.'

'Hmm, well I'm not convinced. I'm keeping an eye on him.'

'Leave him alone, he's been through enough. On that note, if you don't mind, I'd quite like to be on my own for a while.' With that, Aaron placed the earphones in his ears and turned his attention to the screen in front of him where he began looking for something to listen to.

In his peripheral vision he saw his father stand up and hover for a moment, before he walked away. Aaron hoped he had returned to his seat.

CHAPTER TWENTY-FOUR

MELISSA

For a few seconds after Melissa woke up all she remembered was that she was on an aeroplane and they were on their way to Barbados and hopefully, this was going to be the start of a new chapter in their lives. She had smiled to herself as she thought of it, her eyes still closed.

After a moment though, the reality had set in and she remembered exactly what had happened so far on their flight. She groaned and chastised herself for getting involved, why hadn't she listened to her gut and kept quiet? Still, it was done now and in a couple of hours they would have landed and on their way to their hotel and a cold glass of rum punch. Well, rum punch for her and whatever they had for kids for Theo.

Theo.

Melissa opened her eyes and turned to the seat next to her to see what her son was up to while she had slept. He wasn't there.

She sat upright and looked around her. When she still couldn't see him she called his name. 'Theo?'

She bent over to look under the seats in case he'd crawled

under there and fallen asleep, but all she could see was an empty space. She remembered Maggie and spun round on her knees, but the older lady was asleep, her chin on her chest. Melissa's eyes raked up and down the aisle.

'Theo?' This time she raised her voice; people were starting to stare.

Charley appeared behind her. 'Melissa, what's the matter?'

'It's Theo, I can't find him.'

'What do you mean?'

'I mean I was asleep but when I woke up he was gone.' Melissa was aware her tone was aggressive, but she thought Charley's question stupid.

She watched Charley look up and down the aisle as she had done, as if he might appear from nowhere.

'I'm sure he's probably only gone for a wander,' said Charley, lightly. 'Let's walk up and down the plane, I'm sure we'll find him in no time. We'll check the toilets as well, in case he's got himself locked in and can't find his way out.'

Melissa swallowed hard and nodded. Charley was probably right, but she had a sick feeling. What if the murderer had taken him to teach her a lesson for sticking her nose in other people's business? She *knew* she shouldn't have got involved.

'Right, I'll check the toilets at the back of this section and then walk down the other aisle. I'll ask my colleagues to check the other toilets and you can walk down this aisle. Okay?'

Melissa nodded, but she was wringing her hands and trembling.

'Melissa?' She turned as Charley put a hand on her arm. 'We're on an aeroplane, he can't have gone far. We'll find him.'

Melissa relaxed a little as she realised Charley was right. He can't possibly have wandered far, he probably just got bored while his mum and new friend, Maggie, were sleeping. It did seem odd though that none of the other passengers would think there was something wrong with a toddler wandering up the aisle by himself.

She made her way to the back of the plane and began searching. She looked under each seat on either side as best she could without climbing over anyone, or crawling under their feet. She made sure to check each foot space as well, just in case. Melissa could hear Charley knocking behind her, and then the click and swish of each of the toilet doors opening. Charley was gently calling Theo's name and Melissa realised she should probably do the same, he was far more likely to come out of his hiding place if he could hear his mum.

Crouched low, and almost crawling, Melissa made her way down her aisle of the aeroplane. She swallowed hard as often as she could in an effort to quell the nausea she felt. Her mind started to drift to all sorts of terrible scenarios and she knew she was catastrophising, but she couldn't help it.

Get a grip! You're on an aeroplane, he can't have gone anywhere. Even if someone has taken him, they can't very well hide him anywhere for long.

Melissa pushed the thoughts away and focused on her search. She'd probably find he'd made another new friend and was sitting on someone's knee happily munching on whatever snack they had given him. But if that were true, how come no one had brought him back? Or spoken to the flight attendants? Surely any normal person would know that a toddler walking around by themselves was odd – even on an aeroplane. If that was what had happened, what kind of mother did that make her? She hadn't even taught her child about stranger danger.

Tears welled in Melissa's eyes as she sat back. She pressed her hands into her thighs and screwed her face up trying to regain control. She was no use to anyone, least of all Theo, if she had a meltdown in the middle of the aircraft. She sucked in a juddering breath and as she moved to resume her search she heard a tannoy announcement and froze.

Ladies and gentlemen, we are currently searching for a two-year-old little boy who appears to have gone for a wander. If you see him, please contact a member of cabin crew immediately. Otherwise, I must ask you all to remain in your seats for the time being in order to make the search easier. Thank you.

The eyes of the passengers nearest to Melissa all shifted to look at her. She shrank back a little, as if just a look could do her harm. Some of those watching her had faces filled with sympathy, others had their lips pressed together in judgement. She opened her mouth, ready to defend herself and then realised she was wasting time. Both hers – everyone had already made their assessment – and time that could be spent looking for Theo.

Melissa resumed her search, completely ignoring everyone around her. As she arrived at a bulk head she remembered there were more toilets here and that Charley had said she would get the other cabin crew to check them. They probably had already done so, but it wouldn't do any harm for Melissa to have a look by herself. She pushed open the bi-fold door and looked in. The room was tiny and there wasn't anywhere for a small child to hide, it didn't stop her from lifting the toilet lid just to be certain though.

Feeling a little foolish, Melissa continued her search down the aisle, studiously ignoring the glares she could feel jabbing at her.

As she approached the first class stairs, she hesitated and

stood, peering up towards the second floor. How foolish that something as silly as a flight of stairs could halt somebody in the same manner as a brick wall.

Don't be an idiot, you're looking for your son.

With determined steps and putting on a braver face than she felt, Melissa made her way up to the first class cabin. She'd been there earlier of course, but this was different. Earlier she had been invited, this time she was a gatecrasher.

She had expected everyone inside to turn and face her accusingly. For at least one person to demand what the hell she thought she was doing, but everyone was oblivious. So far as she could see, no one had even noticed she was there.

And then it struck her. No one had noticed her because they assumed her to be cabin crew, and the only reason to speak to a member of cabin crew was to ask for something. No one in first class had any reason to walk down the stairs until they had to leave the plane. They did not imagine for one second any of the minions from cattle class would dare to breach their sanctum.

Why was it that Melissa did not feel she could simply crawl along the floor in first class as she had done in economy? She needed to search the same areas and that was the most effective way of doing so.

'Fuck it,' she muttered. The announcement had gone out to all of the passengers, so they must know what was going on.

On her hands and knees she started down the aisle. Almost immediately she realised this was going to be a more difficult search. The first class seats were encased in little pods and she would need each person to stand so she could see under their seat.

She stood and for a few moments considered what might be the best course of action; suddenly she blanched. What if he was hiding under one of the dead women? She'd seen plenty of dead people in her time, it was par for the course when you were a nurse, this just felt entirely different for some reason.

The first class cabin was quite small, there were only eight seats, so it wouldn't take long to search. Despite the fact Melissa had met some of the occupants earlier in the flight, she was not confident enough to ask them to move from their seats, so she decided to enlist the help of one of the cabin crew. She knew there was a bar at the front of the plane, so she made her way forward and hoped no one would challenge her on the way.

Once through the next set of curtains, Melissa found herself in the bar area and stopped, stunned to see how the other half lived – even on an aeroplane. She had never seen so much *space* on an aircraft. She'd only ever seen a plane crammed with rows and rows of seats, some with a couple of inches more leg room than others.

This was a whole new experience and an entirely different atmosphere than she was used to. There was not a plastic tumbler, not a miniature bottle in sight; only glassware and several proper optics. As if having more money meant you were less likely to break a glass and stab someone with it. The bar appeared to be as well stocked as her local Wetherspoons; the difference being, these were premium spirits.

'Can I help you?'

'S-sorry,' she stammered, not quite knowing what to say next.

Melissa recognised the man behind the bar as the flight attendant who had answered her call when she'd put her hand up as having medical knowledge; she couldn't remember his name. His frown deepened as she stood there staring at him and not saying anything.

'Can I ask why you're here? I know your seat is in economy.'

'My son... it's my son who's missing. I'm looking for him, I just need some help.'

'Ah, I didn't realise it was your wee guy,' said the man, his face softening.

'Melissa? What's going on?'

CHAPTER TWENTY-FIVE

AARON

Aaron had spotted Melissa as she made her way through the cabin a few moments earlier. He wondered why she was there. According to Charley, she had made it quite clear she didn't want anything to do with them anymore. Intrigued, he'd waited for her to pass through the curtains and then followed her.

He emerged into the bar in time to hear her tell the flight attendant behind the bar that it was her son who was missing. He'd heard the announcement earlier, but hadn't put two and two together. Why would he? There must be dozens of children on the flight. He'd had a quick look round and checked underneath his seat, although he already knew there would be no one there. He'd not slept a wink for the entire flight and even when he was listening to music, his eyes had refused to relax.

'Melissa? What's going on?'

Melissa jumped and whirled round to face him, her eyes started to fill with tears.

'It's Theo, we can't find him.'

'Can't find him? What happened?'

'I-I fell asleep, when I woke up he was gone. He must've got bored and gone for a wander. I can't believe no one's seen him.' Her words caught in her throat and the tears started to spill down her cheeks. Aaron's heart went out to her and he could imagine the anguish she was going through.

'I, we, need to check under the seats in your cabin. I came to ask...' Melissa turned to the flight attendant.

'Stan.'

'Sorry, Stan. I came to ask Stan to help, I didn't want to do it myself. I thought people might get angry with me.'

'No one is going to get angry with you, I promise,' said Aaron, rubbing Melissa's arm. 'I'll help you. Stan, perhaps you could search in here?'

'Of course. I'll do it now. There are a few little places where he *could* be hiding, but it's doubtful.'

'Please check anyway, if only to put Melissa's mind at rest.' If there was one benefit to having a lot of money – apart from the obvious – it was that people were more likely to do what you asked of them, even if they didn't want to. A power often abused by many who moved in the same circles he did. Aaron preferred to use it for good.

He responded to Stan's tight smile with one of his own before turning his attention back to Melissa.

'Come on, we'll go and search our cabin, make sure he's not hiding under someone's seat without them realising.' He had been trying to keep his tone light, but he could see it was lost on Melissa who just nodded in answer.

She allowed Aaron to lead her back into the cabin and he decided it would be easier to make one announcement and ask them to check their own seat areas.

He stood in front of Melissa and raised his hands in the air, amplifying his voice to be heard. 'Everyone, could I have your attention for a moment please?' Aaron waited until there were four pairs of eyes trained on him. 'The little boy who has gone missing is Melissa's son. Theo has gone for a little wander by himself, so could you quickly check under your seats to make sure he hasn't snuck in and gone for a nap.'

Despite there only being four other people in the cabin, the noise of them standing up and checking under their seats sounded deafening in comparison to the previous quiet. Aaron thought he heard someone muttering about what an irresponsible mother Melissa must be to lose a child and on an *aeroplane*. He turned and glared, but couldn't determine who had voiced their unwanted opinion.

He looked around the cabin, hoping someone would give a small yelp of joy, but he was met with blank faces and shaking heads. Dejected, he wondered what else he could do, where else could the child be? Aaron was getting really worried.

After a few moments, he felt a hand on his arm; Melissa was trying to get his attention.

'Sorry, I was miles away. I can't believe he hasn't turned up yet.'

'It's fine, I was just thinking, what if he's under... you know...' Melissa's eyes darted past Aaron, and he realised what she was getting at.

'You mean what if he's hiding under Mother or Lydia?'

'Yes,' replied Melissa, flushing at having to say it.

Aaron took a deep breath and closed his eyes for a few moments. 'I'll go and check.'

'Thank you, and I'm sorry.' Melissa peered at him with big eyes and he knew she meant it.

He checked under Lydia's seat first, swallowing hard as he crouched down and lifted the corner of the blanket covering her body. Thank goodness he didn't have to look at her face, he rather suspected that might have broken him completely.

There was no sign of Theo under Lydia's seat so he moved on to his mother's, which meant coming face to face with his father.

'Did you check under your seat, Dad?'

'Of course I did, what kind of monster do you think I am?'

'I didn't mean it like that, I'm just double-checking. Melissa's beside herself with worry.'

Both men looked over to where Melissa stood, her arms wrapped around her ribs and tear stains tracked down her cheeks. Her eyes cast about constantly as if Theo might pop out from a secret hiding place and she might miss him.

'I need to check under Mum, just to be sure.'

'I doubt he's there, but you're right, probably best to check, to be certain.'

As they had suspected, there was no sign of Theo there either. Aaron stood back up and shook his head in Melissa's direction. At his signal, she let out a sob and covered her mouth with one hand, crouched over, struggling to stay upright. Aaron dashed over and put an arm on her, helping her to remain on her feet.

'Come on,' he whispered, 'we'll go back into the bar.'

He whisked her through the curtains and sat her gently on the sofa.

'I take it you found nothing?' he asked Stan.

Stan shook his head. 'No, sorry.'

Melissa was wracked with sobs and the tears poured down her cheeks; she had stopped bothering to wipe them away. Aaron sat next to her and put an arm around her, pulling her into him. His own concern for the child rising rapidly.

Charley appeared through the curtain. 'Melissa?'

'Nothing, you?' Aaron answered for Melissa.

'Nothing here either.'

Aaron could feel his temper rising. 'This is ridiculous, a two-year-old child can't just disappear on an aeroplane in mid-air. He must be here, there must be somewhere we haven't checked yet.'

'What if...' The colour drained from Melissa's face.

'What if what?' asked Aaron.

'What if the murderer has him? As payback for me interfering? What if he's hiding him somewhere? What if he plans to kill him too?' Melissa descended into hysterics, unable to say anymore.

Aaron could feel the tears prickle in his own eyes and he blinked rapidly to try to clear them. His emotions already running high, Melissa's tears only made matters worse. 'Let's not think like that, hey? There has to be a reasonable explanation.'

'But there isn't, is there? You said yourself we've searched everywhere. I've lost him, haven't I? This is what I get for being an awful person.'

'You're not an awful person, you mustn't say that. You're a kind and caring person, who just wants to help everyone.'

As he held Melissa, one hand gently rubbing her arm, Aaron wracked his brains to try to think what to do next. He was becoming more and more concerned for Theo's welfare too, but he couldn't say that to Melissa, it would only make her worse.

'I can't just sit here and do nothing,' he said, standing up after a few seconds.

Melissa wiped her face with the tissues Charley had handed to her. 'What are you going to do?'

'I don't know exactly, but I can't just sit here and do nothing. It's not in my genes,' he said, running a hand through his hair. 'I'll... I'll re-search the plane myself. I'll shout his name until he hears me.' Without saying another word, he darted through the curtains and back into the cabin shouting Theo's name as loudly as he could. Aaron didn't care who he woke up or who he upset, he had to find Theo.

He didn't believe whoever murdered his mother and Lydia had taken him – he just couldn't.

CHAPTER TWENTY-SIX

MELISSA

Melissa watched Aaron crash through the curtains and was relieved someone was taking Theo's disappearance as seriously as she was. If only she hadn't fallen asleep. If only she'd made sure Theo was strapped into his seat properly. If only she hadn't agreed to come on this stupid holiday. If only she was a better mother. What must people be thinking of her?

The recriminations tumbled over one another in Melissa's mind and all at once she felt the walls of the plane pressing in on her. She could feel her heart being squeezed and her breaths came in pants. Theo was dead, she was sure of it and it was all her fault.

She stood abruptly, but the whole bar seemed to pitch and roll in front of her. She reached out to grab hold of the bar trying to ground herself and stop the pressure that was bearing down on her, threatening to squeeze her until she popped.

She bent over, still clutching the bar, in an effort to ease her breathing, but it didn't work. She was out of breath and no matter what she did, she struggled to gulp in enough air. She could see a dark haze on the edges of her vision and dots of black flickered before her.

'Melissa.'

She could hear a distant voice calling her name.

'Melissa.'

It was closer now. She looked up and Charley was standing right in front of her, a look of concern etched across her face. Melissa could see Charley saying her name, but it sounded so far away.

She felt a tug on her arm and allowed herself to be led back to the seat, where hands guided her down into it. She felt pressure on the back of her head and someone gently pushed her head forwards and down. More words were being spoken into her ear, she could feel breath on the side of her cheek.

'Breathe slowly, Melissa. Deep breaths and hold them.'

She did as she was told and slowly Charley's voice became clearer and louder.

'You're having a panic attack. Take a deep breath in and hold it. That's right, now breathe out slowly. Keep going, you're doing great.'

A panic attack? That's ridiculous, I've never had a panic attack in my life. But she did as she was told. If it was a panic attack she never wanted to experience another one, it was like the life was being squeezed out of her.

A few minutes later, she felt vaguely normal again, if a little exhausted. Charley was watching her, a small smile on her face.

'Welcome back. How are you doing?'

'Thanks, I really don't know where that came from. I've never had a panic attack before.'

'I've seen so many, and had a few myself, I'd know one from a mile away,' Charley replied with a sorrowful smile. 'Usually it's people who aren't keen on flying. They get themselves all worked up and then don't know how to deal with it.'

'Oh, I hadn't even thought of that. Thank you for helping

me, I really appreciate it. You must think I'm a right mess.' Melissa rubbed at her face, not wanting to make eye contact.

'No, I don't. I think you're a mum whose little boy is missing and is having a tough time coping. I'd be more worried if you were absolutely fine.'

Melissa stood and paced around the bar, her hands on her head. 'What am I going to do? Why can't we find him?' She pushed the tears back down inside. She'd done enough crying and it wasn't helping anyone.

'He's here somewhere, we'll find him.'

'People keep saying that, but we've hunted high and low and he isn't anywhere. I'm going to go and search again. Shout his name like Aaron has and see if he answers to my voice.'

With a plan in mind, Melissa started to feel stronger, her head a little clearer.

She entered the first class cabin and began shouting Theo's name. She continued shouting as she made her way back down the stairs and up the aisle.

'Theo! Theo! It's Mama, can you hear me?'

As she progressed through the cabin, she *felt* rather than saw glares from some of the other passengers, but she couldn't care less. Her son was missing and if they had to be inconvenienced in order for her to find him, then so be it. Having to put up with a bit of shouting until she found him was the absolute least they could do.

As she approached the end of the plane, she could see Aaron chatting to another of the flight attendants.

'Aaron?'

He turned to face her and his expression said it all. 'Nothing, I'm sorry.'

Melissa felt the tears threaten and swallowed them down. 'Me neither. What next?'

Aaron looked thoughtful for a moment. 'Next, we get

extreme. We've searched all the places he's likely to be, but not all the places he *could* be.'

'What do you mean?'

'We need to check the overhead lockers. You could easily fit a child in one of those.'

Melissa felt like she'd been slapped. 'He couldn't get up there by himself, someone would have had to put him up...' She trailed off as the implication set in. 'You think the murderer's taken him too, don't you?' Her voice grew louder.

'I don't know, I really really hope not. But what I do know is, there's no other alternative and he has to be somewhere.'

'But... but we would hear him crying, he would be scared.'

Aaron gripped her shoulders. 'We've got to try, we're out of options otherwise.'

Melissa nodded in agreement and tried not to think about how scared her baby must be if he really was stuck in one of the overhead lockers.

'We'll do an aisle each. I'll do this one.'

Too shocked to speak or even cry, Melissa made her way back down the aisle she had walked up a few moments before and began opening and closing the lockers on either side. Most were jam-packed full of carry-on luggage and duty-free bags. Others had a little more space, and although an empty locker could have easily fitted a child Theo's size, none of the lockers had *that* much space.

She sped up as she went along, quickly realising there was no point in looking too closely. It would become abundantly clear if Theo was in one of them. She imagined the door would feel unusually heavy and her son would come tumbling out if he was in there, desperate for his mother and grabbing out to cling on to her.

Aaron was mirroring her actions in the other aisle. He too was becoming quicker and more frantic with each locker he opened. She could see faces looking up at her, one or two glaring, but most with sympathetic expressions. She couldn't deal with them, she was too fragile and too many people empathising might break her completely.

As she neared the front of the plane, she could feel the emotions welling in her. She knew she wasn't going to find Theo in any of the lockers, but Aaron was right, they had to check, just in case.

Up in first class she checked the remaining few lockers before going back into the bar, no longer caring that her ticket didn't allow her entry. Aaron was already there and shook his head sadly as he took in her enquiring look.

'Fuck! Fuck, fuck fuck! Where is he?' she yelled in frustration.

'We'll find him,' said Aaron enveloping her into a hug.

'You keep saying that, but we've been looking for an hour and he's still not here,' she shouted, wrestling herself free. Aaron looked distraught, but he made no move to try to hold her again.

Melissa paced around the bar, her hands on her head. Occasionally she smacked a hand on her forehead whispering, 'Think, think, think,' to nobody in particular.

'Mama?'

Melissa whirled round as a small child hurled himself towards her.

'Theo!' She flung herself at him and picked him up, hugging him hard and kissing his face all over. 'Are you okay, baby?'

'Yes, Mama,' he said pushing her away.

Melissa set him down on the bench and began checking him for injuries; she turned his hands over, pushed up his sleeves and trouser legs, ran her fingers through his hair. Not really sure what she was looking for, but desperate to know he was okay.

Once she had satisfied herself he was in one piece and there were no cuts or bruises, she asked him where he'd been.

'Nap time,' he replied proudly.

'What do you mean? Where?' Melissa looked up wondering if someone else might be able to answer her questions, realising her son probably didn't have the vocabulary.

She saw Aaron first, a beaming smile all over his face. Next she saw Charley, who didn't look anywhere near as happy, and then a younger member of cabin crew, looking utterly ashamed. Melissa looked back and forth between Charley and the second woman, not understanding what was going on. What *had* gone on.

'Who found him? *Where* did you find him? We searched everywhere.'

Charley, a nervous timbre to her voice, said, 'I think you'd better sit down.'

CHAPTER TWENTY-SEVEN

CHARLEY

Three and a half hours to landing

Charley didn't often feel nervous or anxious. She'd been doing her job for long enough to have confidence in her own knowledge and abilities. However, situations like these didn't arise every day, if ever, and there was no beast fiercer than a protective mama. She had no idea how Melissa was going to react once she explained where Theo had been and how it came to happen. Whatever Jen had done, Charley was in charge and it was down to her to explain. She would deal with the young rookie properly once they were on the ground.

Melissa was now sitting on the bench, her arms wrapped protectively around Theo, but she was staring at the two cabin crew waiting for an answer. Her stare was like ice, it was as if she knew mistakes had been made and she was waiting for them to be confirmed. Charley's stomach twisted, Melissa was not going to be easily pacified. Despite her small stature, Charley knew from her limited contact with Melissa she was a woman to be reckoned with and should not be underestimated.

Jen was virtually in tears, her breaths coming thick and fast. Charley wondered if she was going to have to talk another person down from a panic attack.

'Calm down, lovely. Get yourself a drink of water.'

Jen nodded gratefully and made her way behind the bar, taking deep hiccupping breaths. Charley turned back towards Melissa to see her tracking Jen with narrowed, glowering eyes. She watched as Aaron sat next to them and started tickling Theo and chatting to him quietly about nonsense. She was more than a little surprised when Melissa handed Theo over to Aaron without removing the laser focus she had pinned the two flight attendants with.

'I want to know what the bloody hell's going on here. Something's happened, I can tell by the way you're both acting.'

'I think you need to know, first of all, that this wasn't intentional.'

'What wasn't intentional? Did somebody not look where they were supposed to? Where they said they had? Did *she* miss somewhere?' At this last statement Melissa shot daggers at Jen, and Charley felt sure if looks could kill, this would have done it.

'No, it wasn't quite like that.'

'What was it like then?'

'Melissa,' said Aaron, placing a calming hand on her arm, 'you need to let her speak – it's the quickest way.'

Melissa took a deep breath and closed her eyes for a few moments. Charley watched as her shoulders relaxed and her face smoothed. When she opened her eyes again, they had lost some of their heat. Melissa said nothing, merely quirked an eyebrow indicating that Charley should continue.

'Jen's been on a break, so she wasn't involved in the search. She couldn't have known about it,' Charley continued quickly seeing Melissa was about to interrupt again, 'because she was asleep, upstairs.'

Both Melissa and Aaron's face were etched in confusion.

'Aren't *we* upstairs?'

Charley understood. 'At the back of the plane there is a staircase concealed by a small door, that leads up to a separate area. There are bunks up there for crew to use during their breaks, it means they can get some sleep if they need to. Travelling across time zones like we do can make it difficult.' Charley realised she was babbling and forced herself to get to the point. 'Just before Jen went up she saw Theo toddling up the aisle, no one was paying the slightest bit of attention to him. She picked him up and brought him back to your seats, but when she saw you were sleeping she thought she'd keep an eye on him for you.'

'That still doesn't explain why he was gone for so long though.' Melissa's face was etched with confusion and Charley knew she was going to have to spell it out.

She swallowed hard and her eyes flicked to where Jen stood, her eyes downcast.

'Jen took Theo on an adventure. She showed him the bunk space upstairs and he thought it was wonderful. They both lay down and pretended to sleep, but they actually did fall asleep. When Jen woke up and realised the time, she knew you must be missing Theo by then, so she came straight downstairs, and now we are here.'

Melissa's face was thunderous, but it was Aaron who spoke first.

'Are you telling me that not only did she remove a child from his mother, but that she also potentially put him in danger? I assume there is no stair gate at the top of these stairs? She could not possibly have known that Theo would fall asleep too, what if he'd slipped and banged his head? Do you realise how completely and utterly irresponsible that was? You are supposed to be here for our safety, but yet you put a young child in danger.'

'I-I didn't mean to.' Jen's voice was barely a whisper.

'But you did, and let me tell you, I shall be making it my business to ensure Melissa puts in a formal complaint once we land.'

Jen looked like she was going to throw up and Charley decided to help her.

'Jen, go and sort yourself out and then go and help in economy for the rest of the flight please.'

Without looking up, Jen nodded and said, 'I'm sorry,' as she left the bar.

Charley looked closely at Melissa, still waiting for a vocal reaction. When it came, it was quiet but full of power.

'I thought I'd lost him. I *believed* I'd lost him. I thought I was a terrible mother and all along it was just some stupid little girl not *thinking*. How is it even possible that someone like that could have such an important job? All you lot ever bang on about is how you're not just trolly dollys, but you're actually here for our safety, when she has done just the opposite. She put my little boy in danger and made me think I was a bad mum.'

'No one ever thought you were a bad mum. And yes, it was a bit ill-advised, but she believed she was helping.'

'Helping?' Melissa's tone was dripping with contempt. 'How could she be helping? I thought my son had been taken by a murderer. I will never forget that feeling and I should never have had to go through it in the first place. On what planet did she think it would be okay to remove a child from his mother? *Especially* given what's been going on on this aeroplane practically since we took off.'

Charley could hear the strain in Melissa's voice and knew she was struggling to keep the volume under control, struggling to contain her temper. Charley had every sympathy for her too, she could only begin to imagine what had been running through her head all the while her son was missing. She only hoped that once Melissa had calmed down, she would see no real harm had been done and that Jen had not intended to hurt or upset anyone. She was new to cabin crew and any complaint of this magnitude would only mean her contract would not be renewed after her probationary period. Charley knew for a fact that Jen would never do anything like this again; the lesson had been learned.

'I know what you went through, Melissa, and I am so sorry, both personally and professionally. Obviously I will deal with Jen once we are on the ground, nothing will be gained by me speaking to her while we're still in the air.'

'I want her sacked.' Melissa spat out the words unapologetically and Charley winced.

'I'll help you deal with it once we land,' said Aaron.

'Thank you.'

They had nothing more to say to her.

Charley watched the pair turn their attention to Theo who was becoming a bit bored. These two had only met a few hours previously, but they seemed so natural and comfortable together. Melissa clearly trusted him judging by the way she handed over Theo so easily at the beginning of their conversation. Charley also found it odd that Aaron had just assumed Melissa would want his help – the help of a virtual stranger.

'Can I get you anything?' Charley wanted to be away from the situation, but her training and manners kicked in before she could stop them.

'We're fine, thank you.'

Again Charley found it strange that Aaron had answered for both of them.

CHAPTER TWENTY-EIGHT

AARON

Aaron pointedly ignored Charley as she withdrew from the bar. He did notice, though, that he and Melissa were the only people there. This flight was the weirdest he'd ever been on, even if you removed the fact two important people in his life were dead and most likely murdered. He'd never seen an on-board bar so empty and it was usually always staffed. He also realised the cabin crew, Charley specifically, had become incredibly familiar with him and his family, and Melissa. *Although,* he thought with a sigh, *two people dying and a disappearing child were likely to have some sort of effect.*

At that moment, Darius appeared. He must have been waiting for Charley to leave, Aaron surmised.

'Hey, you found him,' he said with a grin. 'Where was he? I thought you guys had looked everywhere.' Darius pulled his hand sanitiser from his pocket and rubbed a small dollop into his hands.

Aaron glanced at Melissa to see if she wanted to answer, but instead she nodded giving him permission to continue.

'He was in the staff rest area – with a member of the cabin crew.'

'What?'

'True story,' said Aaron before he continued explaining the details.

A few minutes later, the tale was told. Aaron couldn't help but notice Melissa flinching and tensing as he explained what had happened.

'When she woke up and saw the time, she realised she'd messed up.'

'Holy shit! So you mean there's like another compartment up here?' said Darius.

'Apparently so, but from what Charley said it's a fairly small space with a few bunks.'

'Even so, that's really cool.'

'What's so cool?' It was Rex.

Darius's face turned red, he clearly still wasn't comfortable being around him.

'It doesn't matter,' mumbled Darius. 'I'm glad he's okay, I'm going back to my seat.'

Aaron shook his head, all the while watching his father.

'What have I done *now*? I didn't do anything.'

'It's not what you've done now, Dad. It's still what you did. He's a bag of nerves around you – he can't even be in the same room as you. What you did was unforgivable.'

'That's a bit harsh, son. I was only looking out for you.'

'You could've done it a different way,' barked Aaron.

'I think I'm going to take Theo back to our seats now. He's had quite a bit of excitement and I don't think him hearing an argument is going to help.'

'Of course, I'm sorry, I wasn't thinking.'

Melissa offered Aaron a watery smile. 'Say bye bye, Theo.'

The young boy flapped one arm around and shouted 'Bye!' in a way that only small children can get away with.

Aaron grinned and waggled his fingers. 'Bye bye.'

Turning round he saw his father roll his eyes.

'What?'

'Noth–'

Rex was cut off, mid-word, by a yell from the cabin behind him. The two men looked at each other before dashing through the curtain.

On the other side they saw Melissa standing in the aisle, holding Theo tight to her, his head angled away from whatever it was she was looking at.

'What's going on?'

Melissa moved into one of the empty seat pods to give them a better look. If he'd been asked to guess, never in a million years would Aaron have predicted the sight before him.

Darius was on the floor, stuck awkwardly half in half out of his seat area. He was grasping his throat and even from a standing position, Aaron could see his pupils were enormous. It reminded Aaron of the transformation scene in a werewolf film he'd watched a couple of years earlier.

'What happened? Melissa, help him, please!'

Melissa stared at him wild-eyed until Daphne stood, her face fraught and her arms outstretched.

'You help him, I'll take your boy downstairs, he doesn't need to see this.'

Melissa paused, clearly unwilling to give up her son so quickly after he had been found.

'I'll just take him downstairs. I promise.'

Melissa handed him over after a nod from Aaron and got down onto her knees. She grabbed hold of Darius's wrist, presumably to check his pulse.

'His pulse is all over the place and he feels so cold.'

'Hot,' groaned Darius, 'so hot. Not cold. Burning mouth, skin. Hands feel numb.'

Melissa addressed the rest of the cabin. 'What happened? Did anyone see what happened?'

'He came back to his seat and sat, then he half got up, but ended up falling,' Archibald said.

'Did he eat anything? Drink anything when he sat?'

'I didn't see him put anything in his mouth. He did sanitise his hands though, I saw him do that.'

'He did that just a minute ago when we were in the bar though.' Melissa looked confused.

'There's nothing unusual about that. Darius was a complete germ-phobe, he did it all the time. Please,' Aaron was desperate, 'help him.'

'I don't know how, I don't know what's wrong with him.' Melissa closed her eyes and covered her ears as if to block out everything around her.

Aaron couldn't take his eyes off her, desperate for her to think of something. For her to suddenly realise what was wrong and help him. He couldn't lose Darius too, who would he be left with? He had been friends with Darius for years, it would be like cutting off a limb.

Melissa opened her eyes, they were calmer, but she spoke with firm authority. 'Let's get him lying down properly. Does anyone know if he takes any medication? Someone check his bag.'

Between them, Aaron and Melissa shuffled Darius round until he was lying in the aisle and took up position of either side of him. Melissa pressed her fingers into his neck.

'His pulse is so erratic. Darius? Darius look at me, do you have any medication? Have you taken anything?'

'Nothing,' he croaked, shaking his head.

Aaron took his friend's hand. 'Hang on in there, buddy, it's going to be okay.'

'Nope... 's not... can feel it.'

'Stop, just hang on.' Panic was beginning to set in, Aaron couldn't lose someone else to this godforsaken aeroplane.

'Someone go and ask for the plane's emergency oxygen bottle – quickly!' Melissa shouted the last word, before turning back to Darius and speaking softly said, 'Darius, is there... I mean... do you have any last wishes, or messages you'd like us to pass on for you?'

'No!' Aaron glared at her. 'He doesn't need to do that, he's going to be fine.'

'Tell them... got to tell them... the only way.'

'Tell them what?' Rex piped up from somewhere behind Aaron.

'Dad! Not now.'

'Got to tell them, Theo is your son.'

Aaron heard gasps from all around him. His stomach dropped and a thick buzzing sound took over in his ears. The walls of the plane closed in and the small windows became pin-pricks of light. This could not be happening. Not now. They'd worked so hard to keep it a secret. Why would Darius do this to him now?

Why, if he believed he was dying, would he choose to spill Aaron's biggest secret now? What good would it do anyone? Was this Darius's way of getting back at him because his dad humiliated him? It couldn't be, that wasn't his style.

Aaron had all of these questions and more tumbling around in his head, and he had the answers to none of them.

'Why?' he asked, gripping his dying friend's hand harder.

'It's for the best, for all of you, you'll see.'

'No!' yelled Aaron a few moments later when Darius's hand went slack in his. He shook his friend. 'No,' he repeated through blurred vision.

He felt a hand on his shoulder and looked up into Melissa's dark brown eyes.

'Aaron, he's gone. I'm so sorry.' The sorrow on her face only compounded his agony; he folded in on himself and sobbed.

He felt a pair of arms envelope him and he allowed Melissa to hold him, clutching onto her for dear life. He cried not only for his friend, his mum and his fiancée, but also for how his life was about to change now their secret was out.

CHAPTER TWENTY-NINE

MELISSA

Three hours to landing

It was never supposed to be like this, was the refrain that ran through Melissa's mind on a continuous loop. Yes, the identity of Theo's father had been kept a secret, but it wasn't supposed to be that way forever and it definitely wasn't supposed to be revealed this way.

Aaron had promised her they would be together eventually, but in the end she hadn't believed him, mainly because he still planned to marry Lydia.

The more she thought about it though, the more she couldn't bear to let him go without a fight. Melissa had told Aaron she didn't want to know any of the details, but they spoke so often, Aaron would inadvertently reveal small details during their conversation and Melissa was able to piece it together.

Melissa had a friend who lived in Barbados and asked if she and Theo could come and visit for a holiday. She didn't know *how* she was going to convince Aaron to leave Lydia, but she did know she had a much better chance if she was on the same small island as him. She knew what she was doing was akin to a Rachel from *Friends* moment when Rachel flew to London to stop Ross marrying Emily; that might even be where Melissa got the idea from. This was different though, she and Aaron had a son together, that had to count for something.

She'd had the shock of her life when she'd seen him in the airport, and her knees had nearly given way when Theo appeared to recognise him. Although Melissa knew where the wedding was taking place and when, she hadn't known when Aaron and his family were due to fly. Thankfully her excuse was half right – Theo did sometimes mistake two similarly looking people for being the same person.

When Aaron's mother caused the scene at the departure gate Melissa's stomach clenched and she thought she might be sick. If she did win Aaron over, then this horrible woman would become a part of her family. Melissa had calmed herself, remembering they wouldn't be sitting anywhere near each other. There was no way Melissa could afford first class and Vivian wouldn't be seen dead in economy.

Now though, Melissa was sitting on the floor of a first class cabin, on an aeroplane, clutching onto the man she loved as he mourned his best friend. Their secret was out and three people were dead – all in the space of a few short hours. And in even less time they would be landing in beautiful Barbados, its beauty now marred by death, murder, and they would be met by police officers who would want to know the details of what happened before she even got the sniff of a bed or cocktail.

Sometime later, Melissa felt Aaron's sobs lessen and his body began to still. She was grateful, one of her legs had gone to sleep and she was very aware she had handed Theo over to a stranger.

Melissa rubbed Aaron's back. 'Come on, let's get you up.'

He nodded and sniffed, rubbing a hand under his nose.

'We need to pick him up and put him in a seat, we can't leave him there,' said Melissa.

'I'll help.' Rex looked more shocked than anything. Although, Melissa didn't know if that was due to learning he had a grandson, witnessing a death, or a bit of both.

Aaron just nodded and carried out the instructions he was given by his father. Once Darius was placed in his seat, Aaron picked up his blanket and draped it over the man.

'Rest easy, old friend.'

'We need to tell Charley what's happened. She'll need to inform the pilot.' Melissa was trying to think practically.

'I think we're owed an explanation, don't you?'

Melissa turned to see Archibald standing behind them, his face puce and he was trembling with silent rage. She tried to catch Aaron's eye, but his were closed, as if trying to block everyone and everything out.

Finally he opened them again and nodded. 'Yes, I think I owe you and Daphne an explanation, and you, Father. Melissa, why don't you go and fetch Daphne and Theo, and tell Charley what's happened and then meet us in the bar?'

Melissa quickly did as she was told, she wanted to be there to support Aaron while he made his explanations; this wasn't just his fault. It wouldn't be easy, no matter what had happened, she knew he had a lot of respect for the people who might've been his in-laws.

She found Charley in one of the galleys downstairs and would never forget the look on her face when she told her there was a third body in first class. Next she told Daphne all that had happened and explained they needed to go up to the bar.

'Will someone please explain what's going on?' said Daphne as soon as they were all congregated. 'I'm quite sure I've had enough of meetings to last me a lifetime.'

'It seems that Aaron is this child's father,' Archibald blurted out before anyone else had a chance to speak.

Daphne clutched at her throat. 'He can't be. He's only two. Aaron and Lydia were together for years.'

'It's true, Daphne, I'm so sorry.' Aaron hid behind his hands. 'I... we, never meant for anyone to find out like this. To be honest, I've only known for a short time.'

'That's as maybe, but what were you thinking bringing your floozie on your wedding trip? Did Lydia know about this?' Archibald was not going to make this easy for anybody.

Melissa recoiled, feeling as though she had been slapped.

'Let's get one thing straight,' Aaron growled, standing up and towering above everyone. 'Melissa is not and never will be a floozie. I don't care what I've done, you'll not be disrespectful to her, none of this is her fault.'

She offered him a weak smile of thanks, but it didn't stop her from feeling ashamed.

'No, Lydia had no idea about Theo, or Melissa. And since you asked, I did not bring Melissa on my wedding trip. We rarely talked about the wedding, she had no idea where it was going to be and I had no idea she had planned a holiday. We were trying to stay away from each other. We were both utterly shocked when we saw one another back at the airport.'

Melissa decided to be honest. 'That's not quite true...'

'What do you mean?' Aaron asked.

'I did know where it was going to be, and when. Although we didn't talk about it much, you said enough for me to piece it together.' Melissa addressed the rest of the group. 'Aaron's right when he says we were trying to stay away from one another though. He had no idea I was going to Barbados and I had no idea when you were all supposed to fly over. I planned to find him once I was there.'

'You're right, Lydia couldn't have had a clue about either of them, otherwise she would never have gone through with the wedding,' said Daphne.

Rex piped up. 'Oh, what a load of old rubbish. Of course she would have, she was only marrying him for his money, seeing as you two haven't any left.'

Melissa looked in amazement between each of the people stood before her and waited for one of them to say something.

'I don't know what you mean,' spluttered Archibald.

'Oh yes you do, don't think I don't know. Don't think I don't get to hear things just because I'm not "one of you",' Rex replied in a tone filled with contempt. 'If Lydia did know about Aaron's little family, she would have married him anyway and then divorced him for everything that he had, claiming infidelity. Don't you dare try to deny it. In fact, I wouldn't put it past you two to have forced her into it.'

Aaron rounded on Archibald. 'Is this true? Lydia was only marrying me for my money? You mean to say I've put myself through hell and back wondering what to do for the best when all along she never actually loved me?'

Archibald and Daphne exchanged nervous glances. 'It wasn't *quite* like that. Lydia had some doubts, some nerves, like most brides. We just encouraged her.'

'You forced your daughter to marry a man she didn't love so she could keep you in the manner to which you'd become accustomed,' said Rex bluntly.

'You're not exactly blameless in all of this, Aaron. You asked Lydia to marry you, but you then went and had an affair. Doesn't sound very much like you loved her either.' Archibald had recovered and utilised the old adage, the best form of defence was attack.

Aaron stood, shocked for a few moments before he sank onto the bench. 'I'm not sure I really did,' he whispered. 'We'd been together for so long and everyone kept dropping all these hints. I felt like I had no choice, but also, I didn't have any reason not to. Lydia was all I knew and I thought I loved her, I really did. By the time I met Melissa and realised how I really felt it was all too late. I had no choice but to do the right thing, we were too far along in the wedding planning. Could you have imagined mother's face if I'd pulled out? I ended it with Melissa and put her out of my mind, I had no idea about Theo of course.'

'So what changed?' demanded Archibald.

'We bumped into each other again...'

CHAPTER THIRTY

MELISSA

The night out

M elissa closed the front door behind her and let out a sigh of relief. She was out – just. Fearful she might be called back right at the last minute, she hurried up the garden path and turned left towards the main road where she could catch a bus into town.

The previous week when she'd mentioned to Ryan about going out with the girls and asked would he babysit Theo for her, he had been all for it. Said she deserved a break and she worked too hard. Melissa had been a little taken aback he'd agreed so easily, but quickly thanked him and changed the subject before he could renege on the offer. The previous day she reminded him of her planned night out and he was still happy to look after Theo. That evening when he got home from work it was a different matter.

Melissa had just got out of the shower and was applying moisturiser while entertaining Theo on the bed.

'What's going on?'

She turned to see Ryan standing in the doorway, a scowl on his face. Melissa knew immediately her night out was in jeopardy.

'I'm just getting ready to meet my friends. Your dinner's keeping warm in the oven, I'll dish it up when I'm dressed.'

'Forget it. It'll be dry and shrivelled by now, especially with your cooking. I'll order a takeaway. Who's looking after him if you're going out?' He looked to where Theo was playing on the bed, blissfully unaware of the tension in the room.

Melissa held her gaze steady, refusing to look away, but her stomach was in knots. 'You said you would, I asked you last week.'

'Oh yeah. Well, I've changed my mind.'

'What? But there's no one else to look after him and I've told the girls I'll be there.' A thought struck Melissa. 'They all said how lovely of you it was to agree to look after Theo, especially after a hard week at work.' It was a sneaky tactic, but she was fairly sure it would work. Ryan might be nasty to her at home, but he wanted everyone else to think he was wonderful. He positively basked in the glow of their adoration for 'taking on' a child who was not his own. He would know that if Melissa cancelled everyone would think it was his fault.

Melissa watched his decision-making process play out across his face. Which would he think was worse? Acquiescing and looking after Theo anyway, or everyone knowing he'd pulled out of his promise to babysit? Melissa had a sneaking suspicion her plan might work, but he could be so unpredictable, she couldn't be certain. She would worry about the consequences later, because there *would* be consequences.

'Fine, but you're not wearing that,' he said, pointing to a slinky little number she'd planned to wear, 'and I want you back here before midnight.'

Not quite what she'd hoped for, but good enough.

Melissa was on the bus. She texted her friends to let them know she was on the way and her screen filled with texts squealing with joy.

A couple of hours later, Melissa was drinking her fourth gin and tonic and was revelling in a happy buzz. Ryan hadn't texted her once all night, but just in case it was a test, she'd text him a couple of times to check on Theo and make sure they were both okay.

'Melissa! Put your phone down unless you're taking pictures! Theo will be fine, Ryan's not an idiot you know.'

'I know,' said Melissa with a grin, 'I just like to check in on my boys sometimes.' She tried hard to make sure no one knew what Ryan was really like, the fallout if anyone realised how he spoke to her behind closed doors was just too awful to comprehend.

'Anyway,' said her friend, Abi, 'are we hitting The Porthouse tonight, or what?'

'Not me, I said I'd be home by midnight.'

Boos rang out around the table and Melissa laughed. 'What? I do what I say I'm going to do, you know that.'

'We know! But you could always text and tell him you're going to be later,' said Deb.

'You guys go, I'm tired anyway and I've got a double shift tomorrow.'

'All work and no play makes Melissa a dull girl,' said Abi with just enough sarcasm to make Melissa think she might not mean it.

'Come on, it's my round. What are we all having?' Melissa chose to ignore the comment; if she took her friend to task it would only ruin the mood.

When she arrived back from the bar, her friends were putting their coats on.

'What's happening?' she said, setting the drinks on the table.

'We're off to The Porthouse now, get in before it gets busy.'

Melissa checked her watch. 'But it's only ten.'

'I know, but there's happy hour too. You could come for that?'

'I'm not spending a tenner to get into a pub for an hour and a half.'

Abi shrugged. 'Suit yourself.'

Melissa watched in mute shock as Abi lifted the drink she had just bought and downed it in one.

'See ya,' she said over her shoulder as she walked towards the door.

'I'm sorry,' Deb said. And she did look sorry at least.

'Don't worry about it,' Melissa said and Deb took that as her cue she could leave.

Looking at the two drinks left in front of her, Melissa picked one up and sighed before taking a big slug. She'd been damned if she was going to waste drinks and go home early, even if it did mean she was sitting in a busy pub by herself.

'Excuse me, is this chair being used?'

'No, it's all yours,' said Melissa with a wave of her hand, not even bothering to look up.

'Melissa?'

At the sound of her name, Melissa whirled her head to face the stranger. Except, this was no stranger – it was Aaron.

'Aaron,' she breathed.

'Hey.' His smiled was as big and warm as she remembered it. 'Can I sit down?'

'Yeah, of course.'

'How have you been?'

Melissa thought for a moment and then told him all about her job and her life since they had last seen one another.

Before she knew it, it was 11.30pm and she was going to be

late home. They'd talked non-stop since Aaron sat and she'd completely lost track of time. Worse than that, she'd missed the last bus, now she would have to pay for a cab.

'Shit!' she yelled, standing abruptly.

'What's the matter?' said Aaron, his brow furrowed.

'I've got to go, I promised I'd be home by midnight and now I've missed the last bus. I need to get a cab. Fuck! And I need to get to a cashpoint.'

'Wow, calm down. Surely it won't matter if you're a few minutes late?' Aaron took one look at the face she pulled. 'Okay, I'm calling you an Uber on my account. Take my number and let me know you've got home safely if you can.'

Melissa desperately wanted to tell him it wasn't necessary, and to keep up the charade, but she knew this was her only chance of getting home anything like on time.

'Thank you, and I'll try.'

As she walked away she felt a pain in her heart. The hour and a bit had been utterly amazing and she knew what she was going home to would be the polar opposite.

She arrived home that evening with a few minutes to spare and managed to send a text to Aaron while she was in the loo; a text she quickly deleted from her sent items. It wouldn't be the first time Ryan had checked her phone; one night he was convinced the Frank she was texting was some other guy, instead of her boss whom Ryan had met many times.

That night she drifted off to sleep with a mind full of pleasant memories.

CHAPTER THIRTY-ONE

AARON

Some months later

Aaron walked along the busy pavement, smiling and nodding at everyone who walked past him. His heart hadn't felt so light in a long time; he was going to meet Melissa and this time she wouldn't need to rush off. A few days earlier she had texted him to say she had left Ryan for good and she would not be going back.

Aaron's elation turned to sadness when he reminded himself that even though Melissa was free to do as she pleased now, he was not. His wedding to Lydia was still due to go ahead, in fact they were in the final planning stages, and were due to leave for Barbados in three weeks. He knew he had to make a decision, but he saw no way out of marrying Lydia.

It was expected of him, and his mother would never forgive him if he gave up on her dream. She would also never accept Melissa; she would say it was because they were from different social classes and she would call Melissa a gold-digger, but

Aaron knew the real reason was because she was black. Of course his mother would never say anything so rude, but it was the truth of the matter. As for raising a mixed-race child who wasn't his, his mother might well explode at that little detail.

That afternoon was the first time Aaron would be going to Melissa's house, it was also to be the first time he would meet her son. Aaron knew he wanted children in his life, but the idea of being responsible for such a vulnerable little person terrified him; he only hoped his fear wouldn't show.

What was he thinking? He hadn't even decided what he was going to do yet and here he was worrying about his reaction to meeting the child properly for the first time. *But he's a child who could very much become a part of your life.*

As he approached Melissa's house, Aaron tried to shake off the negativity and the doubts. Whatever happened, he knew he wanted to spend that evening with Melissa, and if it was to be the last one, because, frankly, he needed to make a decision quickly, then he wanted to enjoy every moment of it. If all he was left with was a memory, then he wanted to be sure it was the very best memory it could be.

He knocked on the front door and braced himself. It was opened a few moments later by Melissa, a small boy on one hip.

'Hey.'

'Hey yourself.'

'This is Theo. Can you say hello, Theo? Say hello to Aaron.'

'Hey, little guy,' said Aaron taking one of Theo's hands and gently bouncing it up and down. Theo snatched his hand back and hid his face in his mother's shoulder. Aaron looked at Melissa mortified, but she only laughed.

'Don't worry, he's pretending to be shy. Aren't you?' She tickled his belly and he squealed. 'Before you know it he'll be crawling all over you, sitting on your knee and demanding you read him a book.'

'Okay,' said Aaron, not entirely convinced.

'Come in.'

Melissa led him to the lounge, where he perched on the edge of the sofa.

'Here, you take him and I'll get us a drink.' Melissa plopped Theo on Aaron's knee and headed for the kitchen. 'Beer or wine?'

'Eh... wine, thanks,' he replied without taking his eyes of Theo. The boy was watching him warily and Aaron couldn't figure out if he was going to burst into tears or not.

'There's no need to look quite so terrified,' said Melissa, who had returned with two glasses of wine. 'Pop him on the floor and I'll grab him some toys.'

They chatted about everything and anything for the next hour or so. The conversation flowed so seamlessly Aaron was barely aware of the passing time. It was only when Melissa said she'd better put Theo to bed that Aaron realised how late it was.

'You know where the wine is, help yourself to a top-up, I won't be long.'

While she was upstairs Aaron had a nosey around the front room, looking at all the pictures Melissa had lined up. They were mostly of Theo at the various stages of his life, but there were a couple with Melissa in them too. God she was beautiful.

'Right, with a bit of luck, that'll be him for the night now.' Melissa looked at her watch. 'Takeaway should be here shortly too.'

Aaron fetched the bottled of wine and topped up both their glasses.

'Does Theo see his dad at all?' Aaron immediately realised his mistake. 'Sorry, I don't mean to pry. Now I think about it, I'm guessing not, he wasn't exactly a nice guy was he. Of course you wouldn't want to see him or want him anywhere near Theo.'

'What?' Melissa looked surprised.

'Or maybe you think differently and you can separate the two relationships. I don't know. I'm babbling now. Ignore me, forget I said anything.'

'Ryan isn't Theo's dad,' said Melissa slowly.

'Oh, I thought because...' Aaron did not want to finish his thought.

'You thought because Theo is mixed-race, Ryan must be his dad?'

'No... um, yes. Is that an awful assumption to make?'

'Not really, it's pretty fair. But no, Ryan's not Theo's dad. Ryan and I got together after Theo was born. I was alone, vulnerable, depressed and I accepted love, if you can call it that, from the first man who came along. No, Theo's dad is a wonderful caring man, who would never treat me the way Ryan did.'

'So how come you're not with him?'

This time Melissa had no quick answer. She played with the rim of her glass, her eyes not moving from her finger.

'It's complicated,' she said eventually, watching him closely.

'Isn't it always. I've been think–'

'It's you.'

'What?' Aaron jerked to attention.

'It's you. You're Theo's dad.'

Aaron shot to his feet. Melissa's stared at the wall while she swigged back some wine.

'But... I don't... Are you sure?'

'Of course I'm sure!' She was looking at him, her eyes blazing. 'I'm not in the habit of losing track of the men I sleep with.'

'Of course you're not. I'm sorry, I didn't mean to imply...' He sat back down on the sofa beside Melissa. 'It's just such a surprise. Why didn't you tell me?'

'Because I didn't want to ruin your life. You made it very

clear we were never going to be a thing, and I was happy with that. I never thought I'd see you again.'

'So why are you telling me *now*?'

'Because when I saw you that night it felt like fate and if fate brought you back into my life and kept you here, then who was I to argue?' She paused for a few seconds. 'And because I love you and I want you in mine and Theo's lives. I know you're due to get married and I know you've been with Lydia for forever and I have no right to ask. But I feel like if I don't throw my hat in the ring I'll regret it for the rest of my life.'

Aaron stared at her dumbstruck, she loved him? She looked back at him with equal measures of hope and fear in her eyes. She was putting herself out there, and whatever he said next he needed to make sure he meant it, and he used the right words.

'Say something,' she pleaded.

'I'm sorry, this is all just so... unexpected.'

'Unexpected? That definitely wasn't on the list of things I imagined you saying. It's clear you don't feel the same way about me as I do about you. Don't worry, I'm not expecting anything from you for Theo, so you can forget all about him – and me. I think you should leave now.' Melissa stood and went into the kitchen.

For a few moments Aaron didn't move. He was still processing everything, but as he watched her walk away a feeling washed over him. A feeling of longing, of regret, like he may never be happy again.

He chased Melissa into the kitchen. 'I love you too.'

'No you don't, you're only saying that because you think it's what I want to hear.'

'No, that's not true. I realised the moment you walked away from me that I never wanted you to do that again. I'm sorry I didn't say the right thing back there, but I'm saying it now. I love you and I want to be in your life and I want to be Theo's dad.'

'Really?'

'Really.'

Melissa smiled and she threw her arms around him, kissing him fervently.

'What happens now?' she asked when she finally pulled away from him.

'I've got a plan.'

CHAPTER THIRTY-TWO

AARON

Three hours to landing

'So what was your big plan then? Because it doesn't seem to have worked.'

Aaron pulled his eyes from Melissa's to look at Archibald who was still demanding answers.

'My plan was to speak to Mother and get her onside, convince her this was my opportunity to be truly happy in life. And then I would gently let Lydia down. I wasn't convinced she loved me anyway, so I thought there was a chance she would be happy with my decision. I thought if I could explain to Mother about Melissa and Theo and tell her this was the right thing to do and it would avoid a full-blown scandal if it came out, she might just back me.

'Except it didn't quite work out like that. I never got so far as speaking to Lydia. My mother went apoplectic. I completely misjudged her and she refused to support me or give me her blessing.'

'So you killed her. And then you killed Lydia when she refused to postpone the wedding,' said Daphne quietly.

'What? No. Of course I didn't kill my mother, I didn't kill either of them.'

'But it's all rather convenient for you, isn't it? The two people who stand between you and the woman you say you love, and your son, are dead. There's nothing to stop you now from having the life you want.'

'That's all true, but I wouldn't kill to be with Melissa. I'm not a murderer. For God's sake, I didn't even know they were going to be on this flight.'

'Aaron, please tell me you didn't.' He heard the tremor in Melissa's voice, she wasn't sure, she didn't trust him, it was all there in her tone.

'Of course I didn't!' He was shouting, but he didn't know how else to make them listen. 'What about Darius? How do you explain his death? He knew about you and Theo. He was the first person I told after I left your house that night, he supported me. Why would I kill him?'

Aaron couldn't believe this was happening. He'd thought that by being honest there would be no more secrets, but now everyone seemed to think the deaths on the aircraft were not only linked to his relationship with Melissa, but that *he* had orchestrated them. He wracked his brains to think of a way to prove he wasn't responsible.

'I have no idea why you might kill your friend, but I am more sure than ever now I have heard your story that you are at least responsible for Lydia's death, and your mother's. You are the only one who had anything to gain.' Archibald jabbed his finger in the air to make his point.

'I love Melissa, but I wouldn't, *couldn't*, kill anyone just so we could be together. The thought makes me physically sick. My mother was difficult, yes, and I didn't love Lydia in the way you all wanted me to, but that doesn't mean I hated them, or wanted them dead.'

'Why? Why did you have to kill her? Why not just leave her? Split up and let her live the rest of her life?' whispered Daphne, silent tears trailing down her face.

'But I didn't kill them! Melissa, please tell them, you know me, you know I would never do anything like this.' He reached a hand out to take hers, but she shrank away from his touch.

'But I don't know you, do I? Not really, we barely know each other. How am I supposed to know what you might be capable of?'

'No,' said Aaron softly. 'No, not you too. Please, Melissa, I love you. I'd do anything for you.'

'That's the problem though, isn't it? You have done anything for me, but that's not what I wanted. I didn't want to be with you at any cost. I didn't want anyone to die. Yes, I was on my way to try to persuade you not to marry Lydia, but that's not the same as killing people. You promised me Theo would never want for anything, and although I never *asked* for anything, I was grateful to you for offering.'

'I promise you. I *swear* on Theo's life I had nothing to do with this.'

'Don't you dare! You do not get to swear on my son's life for anything.'

Melissa's glare stabbed at his chest and he took a step backwards.

'I can't be here. We're going back to our seats.' Melissa picked Theo up and left the bar.

Aaron stared after her. He couldn't breathe, his throat was choked and tears streamed down his face. He was going to lose everything.

'I think that sums it all up. Daphne, go and fetch that air

hostess, Aaron needs to be restrained and the police need to be waiting when we land,' said Archibald.

'Restrain... what? I haven't done anything.'

'I don't believe a word you say anymore, but the police will decide what to do with you. They'll get to the bottom of it with their forensics and things.'

Aaron could do nothing but stare. There was no point in arguing with Archibald any further, he'd made up his mind and nothing Aaron said was going to make any difference. When Charley arrived, he would speak with her and make her see sense. Restraining him for the rest of the flight was nothing short of ridiculous, there was still three hours to go.

Aaron collapsed onto the sofa and tried to figure out where it had all gone so horribly wrong. And not only that, but who *was* responsible for the deaths and why would they want Lydia, his mother and Darius dead in the first place?

Rex sat next to Aaron. 'How are you doing, son?'

'How am I doing? Really, Dad? It's like I'm living in a reality TV show or something. *I* know I didn't kill them, even though no one believes me, but that still leaves the question of who did. I get how it looks, maybe that's how it was supposed to look? But what have I done to deserve any of this? Who could possibly hate me so much?'

'Try not to worry about it. If it wasn't you, then the evidence will back that up.'

'If? Thanks for the vote of confidence!'

'You know what I mean. I'm on your side. Don't go looking for enemies in places they don't exist. You have enough to deal with as it is.'

CHAPTER THIRTY-THREE

CHARLEY

Two and a half hours to landing

C harley checked her watch, there were still over two hours before she could make everyone sit in their seats. This flight was going down as the very worst in her career. It could not be over soon enough; once they started their descent, she would feel a lot more comfortable and in control.

When she had told Liz about the third body, Liz had immediately ordered the cessation of all hospitality on board. Even though it didn't appear Darius had eaten or drunk anything that caused his death, and no one in economy had been affected, she was not prepared to take any more chances.

The sheer number of 'meetings' and confrontations had left her exhausted. Maybe she would ask to switch to short-haul for a while? There wasn't a bar on short-haul flights and if anything went wrong, they could land somewhere a whole lot sooner.

A minute or so earlier, Melissa had rushed past with Theo on her hip; the poor woman was crying again. God only knew what further revelations had come to light. Charley felt for the young woman, she really did, but she wasn't sure she had the strength to lend her the support she needed. Charley had already become too involved and now she needed to maintain her professional distance. She needed to be in control when the time came to land. Besides, there was that nice lady sitting near Melissa, and Charley was sure she would lend a shoulder to cry on.

Feeling a little shaky, Charley decided to have a quick snack and take a moment to get control of her thoughts and re-centre herself. She took a bite of a KitKat and closed her eyes.

'Excuse me?'

Oh for fuck's sake!

Charley opened her eyes, her professional smile already fixed firmly in place. 'How can I help you... Daphne, isn't it?'

Of course it was, of course it had to be one of *them*.

'Eh, yes. My husband has asked for you to come to the bar please. We believe we know who the culprit is and we would like you to restrain them until we land.'

'Oh, okay, of course.'

Once Daphne had turned her back, Charley chanced another quick bite of her KitKat; she couldn't guess when the next time she would be able to eat might be.

Charley followed Daphne into the bar area where she was faced, once again, with the wedding party, *or what's left of them*. Gallows humour at its finest.

'Ah, there you are. I believe *he* is responsible for the deaths on board and I demand you restrain him for all our safety.'

Charley looked to where he gestured. 'Forgive me, which of the Mr Fortescues are you referring to?' She was pretty sure Archibald meant Rex, but her professionalism demanded she make certain.

'I am *talking* about Aaron Fortescue.'

Charley could not conceal her surprise and asked the man to repeat himself.

'You heard me, I said Aaron Fortescue. It has transpired he had an affair with that girl, Melissa, and he is the boy's father. He has poisoned his mother and our daughter to get them out of the way so he and the girl can be together.'

'Allegedly,' growled Rex from beside his son.

Charley watched Aaron, his head hung low and shaking slowly.

'Are you sure?' Charley was certain there had been some mistake.

'I am as certain as I can be. He is the only one to benefit from their deaths. The police will carry out their investigations, but I am certain they will come to the same conclusion.'

'But what about the young man? Darius, wasn't it?'

'Yes,' Aaron croaked.

'I do not profess to have all the answers, perhaps he was blackmailing Aaron. It *was* Darius who spilled the secret as he lay dying after all.'

'Darius was *not* blackmailing me. He would never do such a thing.'

Charley barely knew what to say. Everything Archibald said made sense, but she could not believe this kind, polite man could ever murder anyone, for any reason. She would have to do something; the Grant-Fernsbys were not going to let it go, that much was clear.

'I– Let me speak to the captain and we'll go from there.'

'And what if he murders someone else in the meantime, hmm?'

'I take your point, Mr Grant-Fernsby, however I will only be a few minutes. Perhaps you could keep him in your sights until I return.' Charley raised her eyebrows to highlight her barely concealed sarcasm. It was apparently wasted on Archibald who only grunted in agreement.

Charley didn't know whether to laugh or cry. At least she didn't need to make the decision. She would however have to enforce it and she could only hope that if Liz did instruct her to restrain Aaron Fortescue, he would allow her to do so without fuss. She knew for certain she would not be happy to be trussed up for two hours based on a vague supposition by a man hurting from the loss of his daughter.

If Aaron did try to resist, she would have no option but to enlist the help of her colleagues and that would only attract even more attention. Attention she didn't want or need, especially if it transpired he was innocent.

Normally Charley would only speak directly to her captain once or twice during a flight, so far she'd managed five times or more.

Charley lifted the handset to her ear. 'Hi, Liz,' she said with mock levity.

Liz was not for fooling though. *'Oh God, what now? Please tell me you don't have another body? This isn't the kind of world record I envisaged holding when I was a child.'*

'No, no. You're quite safe – no further dead bodies, murdered or otherwise, to report.'

'Thank goodness for that. In which case, how can I be of assistance?'

'Some things have come to light and there is reasonable suspicion that Aaron Fortescue is responsible for two of the deaths at least.'

'Aaron Fortescue? The son and groom?'

'Yep. It turns out he's Melissa's son's father. They had an affair, are madly in love – you get the picture.'

'Melissa's son – oh! Jesus wept, that's some plot twist.'

'Yeah, so, Mr Grant-Fernsby has asked us to restrain Aaron

until we land and the police can deal with him. I say asked, it was more of a demand.'

'Right. What do you think?'

'From the very little I know of him, I don't think he did it, but then old Archie is right, he does appear to be the only one to have a motive. *And* Melissa has washed her hands of him, so she clearly thinks he might be involved somewhere too.'

'But he hasn't been aggressive at all, has he?'

'No, not at all. In fact when Archie pointed, I was convinced he was pointing to Rex Fortescue.'

'*Aaron hasn't been rude, or aggressive or a physical threat in any way, so I don't think we can reasonably restrain him. Do you think we could ask him to promise to remain in his seat for the remainder of the flight? Do you think he would agree to that?*'

'That does seem reasonable. It's not as if any of the other first class passengers are going to go anywhere near him now, even if they are basically family.'

'*Let's go with that then. Good luck.*'

Yeah, luck, that's exactly what Charley needed. She couldn't wait for this flight to be over and for a moment she stood and imagined herself lying on the crystal white sands of Accra Beach with a rum punch in hand while she watched the locals play beach cricket. She could almost feel the sun beating down on her face.

Realising she was only putting off the inevitable, Charley stood up straight and smoothed down her skirt.

Back in the first class bar, Aaron was still sitting on the bench, his father beside him. No one was talking, but Archibald was stood in front of them, erect, like some sort of guard. Charley stifled a snort, as if he could stop Aaron if he decided he was leaving.

Charley cleared her throat and they all gave her the attention it demanded. Directing her words towards Archie, she said, 'Since Aaron has not shown any hostility or physical aggression towards anyone and we have no proof of anything, we cannot detain him.' She quickly continued, not allowing any interruptions.

'Having said that, Aaron, I'm asking you if you would agree to remain in your seat until we land? I understand that's not something you would normally *want* to do, but we can all agree these are unusual circumstances. It's only for a short time and assuming you are innocent, the police will be able to confirm that with their tests.'

All three men were staring at her, but she kept her focus on Aaron. It only mattered that he went back to his seat without a fuss. The other two could be handled.

'Fuck off!'

CHAPTER THIRTY-FOUR

AARON

'Dad! You're not helping.'

'You cannot possibly think my son had anything to do with this. It's ridiculous!' Rex was on his feet, leaning in towards Charley.

Aaron stood and pulled on his dad's arm. 'Stop it. Sit down.'

Rex whirled round, his mouth open to speak, but he stopped on seeing Aaron's expression. 'I only want the best for you, that's all I've ever wanted. And now these people are telling all these lies about you.'

'I know, I know, but shouting and getting aggressive isn't going to help.' Aaron could feel his stomach churning, but he knew getting angry would make matters worse. He took deep breaths and calming his father down also helped to calm him. He needed to think clearly. *He* knew he was innocent, but getting angry about it would only reinforce the belief he was guilty.

Aaron watched Rex as he sat, offered a grateful smile and turned back to Charley. Aaron knew she was doing as she was instructed by the pilot to help the other passengers, and the crew to feel safe, and yet despite his words to his father, he wasn't ready to comply easily.

'Am I legally obliged to submit to your request?'

Charley swallowed. 'I cannot force you. I'm not a police officer and therefore I do not have that power. However, the safety of the crew and passengers is my primary concern. The captain is essentially the law while we are in the air and she has asked that you remain in your seat until we land.'

Archibald changed tack. 'Don't make this hard for the girl. Why don't you just go back to your seat and stay there like a good lad?'

Aaron frowned. 'Please stay out of this, Archibald. Your advice is neither welcome, nor required.'

Archibald coughed and blustered, but without actually forming proper words. Aaron had always been the picture of politeness around him and his words would be something of a shock.

'Mr Grant-Fernsby, why don't you return to your seat and check on your wife?' said Charley. 'You have both had quite an ordeal and I'm sure some rest before we land will do you both good.'

'But what about–'

'Please don't worry. I am sure I have nothing to fear from either Mr Fortescue, but it might be easier to talk in private.' Charley looked to Aaron, quirking an eyebrow.

'Of course not. In fact, Dad, why don't you go back to your seat as well? Whatever happens, I'll be through shortly anyway.'

Rex looked as though he was going to argue, but changed his mind. 'Fine, but I'll be consulting my solicitors the moment we land.'

'Thanks, Dad. I'll be through in a minute.'

Aaron watched as his dad left the bar and turned his

attention back to Charley who was standing with her hands behind her, apparently studying the floor.

Aaron cleared his throat. 'Why don't we sit?'

'I'm sorry, Mr Fortescue, but I don't think that's appropriate.'

'Okay, well, do you mind if I say something? If afterwards you still feel that I need to keep the promise you've asked of me then I will do so without question.'

Charley thought for a moment, before silently agreeing.

'First let me start by saying I understand your position and your concerns. This must be the toughest flight of your career and I don't blame you for wanting to try to stop the person who is apparently responsible. However, I would point out to you, that even if I am the killer, it would not matter where I was on the aeroplane, nor if I was restrained.'

Charley started. 'What do you mean?'

'Simply that when my mother, Lydia and Darius were poisoned, assuming that is the case for all three, it was done so at a distance. *If* I am the killer, as Archibald would have everyone believe, then limiting my movements would make no difference. Either I have finished killing *or* the mechanisms are already in place.'

Aaron paused to allow Charley to absorb what he had said. He watched as she stared into the middle distance and he allowed her to be alone with her thoughts.

After a few moments her eyes snapped to his. 'You're quite right in all that you say and I understand asking you to remain in your seat for the duration of the flight might make no difference to any outcome. *But* it would help to make everyone feel a bit safer if I could tell them you won't be moving around the cabin freely.'

Aaron stared at Charley, hard. How far was he willing to push it? Could he make and stick to the agreement?

He gave in. 'I am quite prepared to voluntarily remain in my seat until we land and the police are brought aboard. If I need to visit the facilities then I will only do so with an escort. Will that be acceptable?'

'I–'

'I'm quite sure Archibald will be the first person to shout should I break such an arrangement.'

'Thank you, Mr Fortescue. The police on the ground have already been alerted to the situation.'

'I quite understand, and have no doubt they'll be detaining us all for a while.'

Frustrated at still being thought of as a suspect, Aaron made his way back to his seat, Charley following behind.

'Having spoken with Mr Fortescue, we have reached an agreement that he will not move from his seat for the remainder of the flight.'

'And what if he reneges?'

Aaron shook his head. 'I have given my word, Archibald. I think you know me a little better than that.'

'I thought so, but not now.' Archibald folded his arms and turned to his wife where he whispered furiously.

'I'll move seats, son, then we can talk,' Rex said.

'Talk about what?'

'Everything.'

Aaron was surprised, he couldn't remember his dad ever wanting to talk before. Of course they *spoke*, but it was clear his dad meant something different. They'd never had a particularly close bond, he didn't with either of his parents, truth be told. *Talking* wasn't something he was used to doing with them. Rex was a man's man, and Aaron had grown up believing his dad thought talking was a frivolous activity undertaken by women.

Aaron lowered himself into his seat and leaned back with his eyes closed. *What an absolute nightmare.* How could so much have changed in just a few short hours, and at 30,000 feet?

CHAPTER THIRTY-FIVE

MELISSA

One and a half hours to landing

Back in her seat Melissa's inner monologue would not be still. She kept asking herself, over and over, how had she got it so wrong? How was it possible she had fallen for another awful man. Ryan was a lot of things: patronising, a bully, manipulative, but he was no murderer. Aggressive and scary at times, but he had never laid a finger on her. He'd never had to, the fear kept her in check.

Aaron had been kind, loving and understanding. How was it even possible he was a murderer? Melissa supposed you could look at it from a romantic point of view. Aaron was willing to kill his nearest and dearest so they could be together. But that kind of rationalisation made her just as warped as him, surely?

She would never have expected him to do something like this, this was... too much. Supposing he had done it and then Melissa decided a couple of years down the line it wasn't working and she wanted to leave. What then? Would he let her leave knowing he had killed two, maybe three, people so they could be together?

Melissa felt as though she was trapped and the air around her compressed her ribs. She needed to get off of this fucking aeroplane. Eight hours was a long time when you were sitting doing nothing, but equally it was such a short space of time when you considered three people had been murdered since they'd left Heathrow.

She folded herself into her seat, screwed her face up and, fists balled into her eyes, screamed silently. God, what she would give to be able to do that out loud. Maybe once she was there, under the water where no one could hear her and she wouldn't scare Theo.

She glanced over to where Maggie was entertaining Theo again, and wondered how she would ever be able to thank the lady. Wondered if she would ever even see her again. Once more, she marvelled at the kindness of strangers. Giving Maggie a small smile, Melissa returned to her thoughts.

Even if you could *somehow* wrap your head around the fact Lydia and Vivian had been murdered for a good reason, and Melissa really couldn't, that didn't explain why Aaron would kill his best friend. Yes, Aaron had been somewhat taken aback finding out Darius was in love with him, but Aaron had always known Darius was gay.

There was no way Aaron would be even remotely upset by something like that, let alone angry enough to kill him. Melissa knew from what Aaron had told her that Rex and Vivian were homophobic, and she would have expected a level of aggression from Rex had he found out a man was in love with him, but not Aaron.

Melissa went round and round trying to find a valid reason for Aaron to want to kill Darius, but she couldn't think of a single one. And while she knew killing for love was not unheard of, the Aaron she knew and loved, or thought she did, was not capable of such a thing. He was the kindest most caring person she knew, and that was saying something given she worked with a whole host of doctors and nurses. It made no sense for him to want to kill Lydia and Vivian, let alone actually do it, in mid-air, somewhere over the Atlantic.

'Are you all right, pet?'

Melissa opened her eyes and turned to look at Maggie. Theo was sitting quietly on her lap, one of his books resting on the table.

'Yes. No. I don't know.' Tears welled in Melissa's eyes. *How do I have any tears left to cry?*

'Do you want to talk about it? I'm a good listener.'

Melissa thought for a moment. Who else was she going to talk to? And she needed to talk to someone, but the thought of all these other people listening in horrified her.

Maggie appeared to know exactly what she was thinking. 'How about I come and sit over there, then we can have a nice quiet chat.' Maggie gestured behind her with her head, her eyes wide.

Melissa managed a wan smile and nodded in agreement.

'I don't really know where to start, to be honest,' said Melissa once they resettled themselves. 'It's all so unbelievable. I can hardly believe it myself. You know when I went up to first class near the beginning of the flight? Well, someone had died and I offered my assistance as a nurse.' She was whispering, not wanting anyone else to hear what she was saying.

'Oh my goodness, that's awful!'

'As it turns out, the woman who died was Theo's grandmother, but she never knew. Her son is Theo's father and I had no idea they would even be on this flight until I saw them at the departure gate. That woman was so incredibly rude to me and she had no idea who I was.'

'But, I don't understand, how could you not know Theo's father would be on the flight? And weren't they all part of a wedding party?'

'They were,' said Melissa before telling Maggie, this complete stranger, all about her life before the aeroplane took off and everything that had happened while they had been in the air.

It felt good to be able to tell someone else, someone who wasn't involved and might be able to look at things more objectively. Even poor Charley was stuck in the middle of it all and she was only trying to do her job. A difficult job at the best of times, but Melissa was sure these last few hours were amongst the most stressful of Charley's career. Melissa's heart went out to the woman whom she thought had conducted herself professionally given everything that had been thrown at her.

By the time Melissa had finished her story she had watched Maggie's face emit every possible emotion. Melissa stopped talking and waited for Maggie to speak.

'I-I'm not sure what to say to all of that.'

'Now that I've said it out loud like that, it is a lot, isn't it?'

'That's one way of putting it. What are you going to do now?'

'Well, I still have a holiday to enjoy, or at least try to enjoy. After the police have spoken to me, that is. My friend obviously knows nothing about what's been going on and will demand to be told everything once I explain I need to speak to the police before I can go to her place.'

'I meant more in the long term. What are you going to do once you go home?'

'What do you mean? I go back to my life as it was before Aaron, but after Ryan. It wasn't so bad. We were happy, weren't we, baby?' Melissa smiled at Theo.

'Will you be happy again though? Knowing what you're missing out on?'

'Missing out on? Aaron likely killed three people. I don't want to know someone like that and much less, I don't want Theo to ever know that's the kind of man his father is.'

'Do you really believe that though?'

'Which bit?' Melissa had thought Maggie would listen to her story and empathise with her, not ask her questions she wasn't ready to face up to yet.

'Do you really believe Aaron is responsible? I've never met him and I only know what you've told me, but it doesn't sound to me like the kind of man who could do something like that.'

Melissa could do nothing except stare at the woman.

'Before this all happened, would you have honestly thought he would kill anyone?'

Melissa thought about the question. *Would I?* 'Before we got on this aeroplane, no, I wouldn't have even considered it.'

'So ask yourself, what's changed? A man you don't know, who is hurting after the death of his daughter, has accused the man you love of murder and *now* you think he might be capable?'

Clarity dropped into Melissa's brain like the proverbial penny. 'Oh my God, you're right. Why would I believe someone I don't know over Aaron? How could he ever forgive me for doubting him? I need to speak to him.'

Maggie looked at her watch. 'Go on then, you won't have long.'

Melissa stood and took a few paces up the aisle before turning round. 'Could you–'

'I've got him, you go and sort out his daddy.'

CHAPTER THIRTY-SIX

AARON

Checking his watch for the millionth time, Aaron gave a low groan of frustration. He'd agreed not to leave his seat, and he didn't *need* to leave his seat, but because he couldn't all he could think about was getting up and walking around.

He needed something to distract himself with until they landed. Until then, nothing was going to change. Failing a small miracle, he would need to wait until they were on the ground and with the police before he could prove his innocence. He *had* to prove he hadn't killed anyone, he was certain that was the only way he could win over Melissa. And if he wanted them all to be a family, she was the one he needed to convince.

At first he'd been hurt and angry when Melissa walked away; she clearly believed every word Archibald had said. He couldn't quite believe she thought it possible of him, but as she pointed out, she didn't really know him very well. Yes, they had a son and they believed in their hearts they loved each other, but they hadn't spent very much time together. He was determined all that would change as soon as he was cleared.

Aaron thought through the events on the plane, looking for

some tiny thread he might be able to tug on to prove he wasn't a killer. His mum's drugs had been tampered with and Melissa thought Lydia had been being poisoned for quite some time, neither of those circumstances helped his cause. No one was very sure how Darius had died, so that was no help either.

If they had all been poisoned as suspected, then there was the argument that it was more likely to be a woman who killed them. Wasn't there some theory or other that poison was several times more likely to be chosen by a woman than a man as a weapon of choice? If that was the case then who were the suspects? Daphne? Why would she kill her own daughter?

Melissa? That made even less sense. If Melissa did this so they could be together then why abandon him after he was accused? Apart from that, she was a nurse, they had a moral obligation to save lives. But she *was* a nurse, surely that meant she had a working knowledge of poisons?

Stop it! Aaron berated himself. *You know it's not Melissa!*

Neither his father nor Archibald had any reason to want all three of them dead, at least none that were obvious. Who else did that leave? There wasn't a single other person on the flight who knew them, as far as Aaron was aware. Scratch that, who else did he know anywhere who might want them all to die and for Aaron to take the blame? If he couldn't prove his innocence he *would* end up in prison and there would be no more family for him.

'I don't care, I want to speak to him.'

'I'm sorry but that won't be possible. First class is only for those passengers holding a first class ticket.'

There was a snorting sound. 'Didn't seem to bother you when you had me here checking out dead bodies for you.'

Melissa? Aaron turned round in his seat trying to see what was going on, but all he could see was the top of the stairs. He made to stand and then remembered he wasn't allowed to leave his seat.

Rex caught his eye. 'I'll go, son, find out what's going on.'

Aaron sat properly in his seat and waited; in his peripheral vision he could see Archibald and Daphne turning to see what the commotion was. He kept his eyes dead ahead and after a moment, could hear the deep rumble of his father's voice. He was speaking quietly, but there was no mistaking his intonation.

Aaron heard footsteps coming towards the cabin. He stood and turned in his seat space; he'd given his word and he didn't want to break it. He was right, it had been Melissa he heard, but why was she here?

'I need to talk to you...' Melissa looked around the cabin, her eyes stopping on Archibald who had already risen. 'Privately.'

'Absolutely not! I will not allow him anywhere near anyone else. You have already seen what he is capable of.' Archibald was clearly not used to being questioned or disobeyed.

Melissa turned to where Charley was standing behind her. 'You said he has given his word he would not leave his seat unless accompanied?'

'That's correct.'

'Fine, I will accompany him to the bar. It's imperative I speak with him immediately.'

'I really—'

'I don't know you, Mr Archibald, and you don't know me, which means you have absolutely no right to tell me what I can and cannot do. I am a grown woman and a mother, which means I am capable of making my own decisions.'

'But—'

'No.' Melissa held her hand up as she spoke and turned back to Aaron. 'Shall we?'

Aaron had never seen Melissa like this, but he had also

never loved her more. He'd seen her spoken down to and patronised, something she usually rolled her eyes at before she moved on. Seeing her stand up to a man twice her size made his heart swell with pride.

He glanced at Charley making sure he had her blessing before he followed Melissa into the bar. As he walked he could feel his father move behind him. At the curtain he turned to face Rex. 'No, Dad. It needs to be just us.' He dropped his voice. 'I won't hurt her.'

Rex looked wounded. 'I know you won't. I'll be here for you when you're done.'

Aaron closed the curtains and gave himself a moment to breathe before turning to face whatever music it was Melissa had brought for him. He had no idea what she might say; hadn't she said it all earlier before she'd left?

'Please, sit down.' Melissa placed her hand on the seat next to her, her eyes imploring.

Aaron did as she asked and waited for her to speak. This was her party and he wasn't about to crash it. She watched her hands lying in her lap as she played with her fingers. He wished she would look at him, just so he would have a clue what she was feeling. Because he had no idea and the feelings were all getting too much.

As he was about to break the silence and his promise to himself, she lifted her eyes to his. God she was beautiful.

'I wanted to–' Her voice broke and she swallowed before continuing. 'I'm here to apologise for doubting you.'

What? But before Aaron could say a word, she continued.

'When Archibald accused you of killing everyone his reasoning made perfect sense to me and all I could think was I needed to get away. I needed to get Theo away.'

'But–'

Melissa held up a hand as she had done a few minutes before to Archibald. 'Please, I'm not finished. All I could think was that I'd made another mistake when it came to men. That I'd left one vile man, one awful relationship, and walked straight into another. I knew I couldn't deal with all of that again, so I ran, basically, well, as much as you can run on an aeroplane. But then I got chatting to Maggie–'

'Who's Maggie?'

'Oh, she's a lady sitting near us. She's been taking care of Theo while I did... all of this...'

'I wondered where he was.' He hadn't wondered at all, what kind of father was he? But it seemed like the natural thing to say.

'That's not important – I mean right now. What is important is I know, deep down, you could never kill anyone and I'm sorry I let a stranger try to convince me you could.'

Aaron couldn't believe what she was saying. 'Do you really mean that?'

'I do. I'm so sorry. Please forgive me?'

'Of course I forgive you.' Aaron leaned forward and took Melissa's face in his hands, gently placing a kiss on her lips, his heart soaring when she responded.

'I've been trying to work this all through in my head. I can't think who would want them all dead, or who might want to frame me for their murders.' He went on to explain his various theories to her. 'Nothing makes any sense.'

'No, it doesn't.'

Melissa leaned in to him and he allowed himself to enjoy her warmth for a few moments. All too quickly they would both have to go back to their seats and when they landed he would still be detained by the authorities. Knowing Melissa believed him made him think he might just be able to cope after all. Thank goodness she had managed to get away from that nutter of an ex of hers.

Sudden clarity.

Aaron sat up slowly. 'What if...'

'What if, what?'

'What if this is all down to your ex? What's his name? Ryan.'

Melissa screwed her face up. 'No, he was a vile human being, but I don't think he'd kill anyone, certainly not deliberately anyway.'

Aaron grabbed hold of her hands. 'But it makes sense, he kills three of the people closest to me in my life and frames me for their murders, which means I go to prison and we could never be together.'

'But how would he even know who you were? Who your family were or where you lived?'

'It's not without its problems, but it is possible. He could have followed you, been spying on the house, then followed me.'

'Maybe, but I think I would have recognised him if he were on the aeroplane.'

'Not if he'd disguised himself and bought a fake passport.'

Melissa shook her head. 'That's quite far-fetched, don't you think?'

'It is, but what other options are there? And far-fetched doesn't mean impossible.'

'It doesn't, but I really don't think Ryan cares all that much anymore, I haven't heard from him for ages.'

'But maybe that's all connected. You haven't heard from him because he's been watching us and coming up with a plan and he's thinking along the lines of, if he can't have you then no one can.'

'But why not just kill us? Surely that would be easier?'

'It would, but in his sick mind perhaps he thinks this will hurt us more?' Aaron suggested.

'Okay, assuming your theory is a possibility, what can we

do? No matter what, we'll still have to speak to the police when we land and they're still likely to arrest you.'

'Very true, but what if he's on the flight and we can give them an alternative suspect?'

CHAPTER THIRTY-SEVEN

MELISSA

Could Ryan really be behind all of this? Could he really be here on this aeroplane?

Melissa wasn't so sure, but she tried to follow Aaron's logic anyway. He was right, it was *possible* and the only valid theory they had. She owed it to him to follow it through and at least ask Charley to check the passenger manifesto. If he was using a fake name, maybe reading the list might spark a familiarity in Melissa's mind. 'Okay, I think we should at least check it out.'

Melissa couldn't help but reciprocate Aaron's broad smile.

'We should ask Charley to look at the list of passengers… what?'

'You need to go back to your seat. If he's using a fake name, I'm the one likely to recognise it and you need to keep your word.'

Aaron slumped. 'I suppose that does make sense.'

'If nothing jumps out, then I'll walk the plane and see if I notice anyone I recognise.'

'I don't want you to do that, what if he realises what's happening?'

'What's he going to do? Jump up and attack me? With all those people around? Doubtful.'

'I still don't like it.'

Melissa laid her hand over his. 'I'll be fine.'

Melissa escorted Aaron back to his seat, promising she would return soon, and then left to find Charley.

'Everything okay?' asked Charley when she saw Melissa coming.

'Everything's fine. Sort of. Do you think I could look at the passenger list?'

'I don't know...'

'I know it's supposed to be private and data security and all that, but I think these can be called exceptional circumstances.'

'Why don't you tell me the name you're looking for and I'll tell you if it's there?'

'Ryan Welford.'

Melissa waited patiently as Charley checked the list and nodded thoughtfully when she responded with a shake of her head.

'The thing is, I think he might be travelling under a false name.'

Charley stared. 'That's ridiculous, this isn't a film. And why do you need to know if this man's on board anyway?'

'He's my ex and we think he might be behind all this.'

'Like I said, this isn't a film and no one apart from my staff, you and the wedding party have been in that cabin. So no, I won't let you look at the passenger list.'

Charley's clipped words stung, but Melissa could see her point. She was unwilling to give up just yet though, she could still cast her eye over each of the passengers. She felt she would know if one of them was Ryan in disguise, she'd lived with him for long enough.

'What's going on?'

'Rex! I didn't hear you coming.' *Everything's so muffled on a plane*, thought Melissa.

'Aaron asked me to make sure you were okay and help if I could, but he didn't say what with, just told me to come after you.'

Melissa quickly filled him in, reasoning she could trust him if Aaron had asked Rex to help her.

'Okay, have you got a picture of him? I'll help you search – we'll take an aisle each.'

'On my phone. It's back at my seat.'

Melissa could see Maggie watching her progress as she made her way up the aisle. She gave a little shake of her head and Maggie nodded to say she understood.

Pulling out her phone and switching it on, Melissa had to navigate to Facebook and unblock Ryan so she could show Rex a picture from Ryan's profile. She'd deleted every picture she had of Ryan when they'd split up, the blocking had come later.

'Right, got it,' said Rex after studying the picture for a short time. 'I'll take that aisle, you take this one.'

Melissa made her way back to the front and started walking up the aisle looking at each of the passengers in turn. At first she ignored the women but then thought there was nothing to stop Ryan dressing up as a woman. *Apart from his pride.* No, he was the walking talking definition of toxic masculinity.

She concentrated her efforts on the men, specifically their eyes. He would struggle to change their shape and she couldn't believe he would resort to contact lenses to change the colour. She received some odd looks and she replied with a smile trying not to piss off anyone unduly.

After walking the length of the first aisle, she blew a kiss to Theo and smiled at Maggie, but there was nothing to report. A quick look over to Rex confirmed he hadn't found anything either.

Melissa returned to first class feeling dejected.

Aaron must have been waiting for her to come back, as soon as she stepped into the cabin he was on his feet, his face expectant. She shook her head and he sat heavily.

Melissa rushed to his side and crouched to his eye level. 'I believe you when you say you didn't kill anyone and the forensics will prove it. I know it'll be shit when we land, but it was going to be shit even if you weren't a suspect, this is just going to take a bit longer.'

Rex nodded. 'She's right, son. It'll all be okay.'

'But what if they don't find any forensics? If Lydia was being poisoned at home they'll need to get in touch with the UK police. Will they allow me to go home while they investigate, or will I have to rot in some Bajan jail? If it goes to trial, Melissa, you'll leave me, I know you will and I wouldn't blame you. Why would you hang around?'

'That's not going to happen and even if it does, I'll wait for you.'

'What, you'll wait twenty-five years for me? Theo will be a man by then and he won't want to know his murderer father.'

'Stop talking like that! We both know you didn't do it and we have to believe there will be evidence of that.' Melissa placed her forehead against Aaron's. 'Don't give up, not before we've even started.'

Aaron nodded his head against hers, but she knew she'd have to be there for him. He needed someone to fight his corner, someone who believed in him, more than one person if possible.

Melissa broke away and fixed Rex with a look. 'Rex, you believe him, don't you?'

'I do,' he said quietly. 'I'll be there for you too, son, and we'll make sure you get the best lawyers.'

Melissa continued, 'I'm going to stay here for a bit, just until we need to land anyway. Theo will need me.'

'That is completely–'

'Shut it, Archie.' Rex's growling Glaswegian accent had returned, but this time Melissa was glad of it.

CHAPTER THIRTY-EIGHT

I think I've made a mistake, which is not something I do very often and something I am even less ready to admit to. And I'm not talking about killing people either, they deserved to die. Well, the first two definitely did, the third, perhaps not. Darius knew too much and I couldn't take the chance he would blab. Just look how he came out with that little nugget about Aaron being Theo's dad. No, I didn't want to kill him, but he left me no choice.

No, the problem here is, it didn't occur to me that anyone would suspect Aaron. I mean, why would they? He's the perfect man – apart from the whole 'having an affair and fathering a child by another woman' thing. Okay, so he didn't know he was a father until a few weeks earlier, but he knew he *could* have been, if you catch my drift.

The annoying thing is, if anyone who knows him actually thinks about it, they'll realise it couldn't possibly be Aaron. He knows *nothing* about chemistry and he's never read an Agatha Christie book. Said something about newer writers and indie authors needing the money and she's dead so she doesn't. He never has liked the classics. I wonder if he *had* read them if he would know, if he would realise who's behind it all, because he really doesn't have a clue.

I almost tried to stop them when he sent Melissa looking for Ryan. He is no longer a problem, let me tell you. He's another one who would never let them live in peace if he'd still been around. Vile, nasty little man.

Because that's why I did all this. That's why I decided to use my knowledge – for good. So my son could have a life with the woman he loves, and their son, without anyone interfering. Because I know what that's like. I know about having to live the life I'm told to and having to behave as I'm expected to, and there was no way I wanted my son to have to do that too.

If anything, I should have interfered earlier. Spoken to him, explained to him how much happier he would be doing what he believed in his heart. It would have meant going toe to toe with Vivian, but that wouldn't have been the end of the world. We hadn't been in love for years and she spent most of her time ignoring me anyway, and that is precisely what I wanted Aaron to avoid.

I realise I'm not making much sense here, so I'll start from the beginning.

When Vivian and I met we were young, dumb and very much in love, or should that be lust? When we were teenagers pre-marital sex was more than frowned upon, it was virtually forbidden. Actually, I should say, it was for *women*, specifically women like Vivian. (No one gave a shit about some Glaswegian guy from the east end.) Vivian was expected to keep her virginity for marriage, otherwise no 'good' man would ever want her. It was all about class and social status and, quite honestly, a load of old guff.

One night, Vivian and I got carried away, as was always likely to happen. After that, there was no stopping us and protection was the last thing on either of our minds. Until afterwards when we would both swear we would be more careful next time – it never happened. Until one day, it was too late. Vivian was pregnant.

I could tell there was something wrong straight away and when she explained she'd missed her period, maybe even two, she never kept count, I panicked. I loved her, but was I *in* love with her? I wasn't so sure. I begged her to get an abortion, but back then your doctor knew you personally, knew your parents and patient confidentiality was far less strict. She had no choice but to tell her mother and father and hope to God they helped her instead of kicking her out.

They gave her – us – two options: get married or get out. And when they said 'get out' they meant it. No home, no family, no friends and worst of all, in Vivian's eyes anyway, no money or inheritance. For Vivian, there was only one option.

I was swept along for the ride, never really appreciating what I was getting myself into and focusing on money. I knew there was money, it was so obvious from the clothes, the cars, the houses. (And yes, I do mean plural – houses.) I'd never had money, our family lived payday to payday and sometimes it didn't even stretch that far. I was blinded by wealth.

Before I knew it, I was having lessons on how to change my accent, how to speak, how to conduct myself at parties, at the dinner table. I changed, literally. The wedding was extremely quick, there wasn't much time if we were going to call the pregnancy a honeymoon baby.

Once the fuss of the wedding, the honeymoon and then the birth of our child was over I realised my life was empty. I'd left all my friends behind, I couldn't make new ones because any who were deemed appropriate knew where I came from. We had maids, and gardeners and a nanny, so there was nothing for me to do, and I knew sure as hell, my wife didn't love me. Our wedding and our marriage were all for show. I swore I would never let that happen to our child, to our boy.

When Aaron and Lydia got together, I didn't think much of it. I couldn't imagine them ever getting married and although they went out for a long time, I was relaxed. Aaron didn't look like he was ever going to pop the question, despite the not-so-subtle hints being dropped by everyone else around him. When he finally succumbed I started to worry and spent all my time trying to figure out how I could put a stop to it.

Then, as often happens, a chance event spilled the answer into my lap – or so I thought. When I caught Darius wanking over a video of Aaron, I wondered if I could somehow use it to my advantage. Not that I thought for a second my son might be gay, it was more about leverage. Knowing Aaron told Darius everything, I made him spill the beans on Aaron and Lydia's relationship. And out came the story of Aaron and Melissa.

The way Darius spoke about them with regret in his voice made me realise, not only did he truly love Aaron, he also knew Aaron truly loved Melissa. I forced Darius to be my source and tell me everything that was going on in their relationship so I could try to find a way for them to be together. When he told me about Theo, about my grandson, I knew I had to act, and I knew I had no choice.

Aaron had the chance to be happy and have the life I never had. If his mother had known, she would have forced Aaron to have nothing more to do with his family, or risk being cut off. If Lydia had found out beforehand she would have married him regardless and then she would have divorced him and taken every penny she could. Not least so she could pass a sizeable chunk on to her near-bankrupt parents. If she'd found out afterwards, the outcome would have been the same.

I had no choice, if I wanted Aaron to live the life he deserved, if I wanted him to be happy, happier than I had ever been, I had to act. It wasn't even a difficult decision – don't all parents want their children to be happy?

Even my weapon of choice was an easy decision. There isn't a lot I don't know about poison and how to administer them. No one knows how good I was at chemistry at school, because no one cared enough to ask. And, to be fair, the victims helped me out with their vanity and their strange little addictions.

I spiked Vivian's powdered painkillers – that was easy. Dropping thallium into Lydia's food was just as easy since she was always eating at our house. Once I realised, on board the plane, that drastic measures were needed, handing her a bottle of water containing the fatal dose was child's play.

Darius's obsession with hand sanitiser made my life extremely easy. As soon as he couldn't find his bottle – because I'd stolen it from his bag – he was only too eager to accept a spare bottle I carried with me. Only my bottle contained aconitine, or as you may know it, Wolfsbane.

Was it worth killing four people for my son's happiness? Absolutely. (Yes, it was four, I pushed Ryan in front of a train at a busy railway station, no need for finesse there.) But I never, ever meant for Aaron to be a suspect, and I am not convinced forensics will help him. The police will not find any fingerprints and I flushed all of the packaging, rubbish and plastic bags down the toilet. I can't imagine anyone even considering checking in the sewage tanks.

That only leaves me with one option.

CHAPTER THIRTY-NINE

Despite being sad that I'm going to have to give myself up, I'm also incredibly proud of my work. If it weren't for the fact I cannot allow Aaron to take the fall for something I did, I'm pretty sure I'd have got away with it.

In dear old Vivian's case, she did the deed for me in a way. I used something you'd likely have in your fruit bowl in the summer, something you would likely have in your mouth and not even realise it could kill you.

Cherry pips.

Any old kind will do, but I wanted to be sure, so I used the very best. Maraschino pips. As few as four or five of these bad boys crushed up would be enough to bring on cyanosis. So I used six, just to make sure and knowing they wouldn't be taken all at once, but would be close enough together to induce heart failure.

You see, dear old Vivian – I call her that because she *hated* to be called old – was very much a creature of habit and routine. Even when she was told something was bad for her or there was a new, better way to do something, she insisted on sticking to her guns. Which is why it was so easy for me.

I stole her box of powdered painkillers from her bag while she wasn't looking. Then I carefully opened two of the papers and sprinkled the cherry pips evenly in each. It had taken me a long time to crush the pips finely enough, but even then they still had a darker hew than the powder. I was confident she wouldn't notice though. She didn't like to be nagged about taking them, so she would pour the contents into her mouth and then swallow a mouthful of water as quickly as possible, hoping no one would notice.

Vivian took these painkillers so often she was like a smoker with a packet of cigarettes, never really concentrating on how many were left and always having a spare pack around. So when I replaced the now-adulterated powders back in her bag, I knew she wouldn't be surprised to find there were only two left. I had to remove the others to be sure she took both contaminated packets close together.

How did I know she would do that?

Because Vivian doesn't take painkillers to kill pain, she takes them as a comfort blanket when she's stressed. And there is nothing more stressful to Vivian than being unable to control things, and travelling was the ultimate in losing control for her.

I could've clapped with delight when she started arguing with the ground staff at the gate. It was typical Vivian and I knew without a doubt she'd be taking a powder before long.

But why did Vivian have to go, I hear you ask? Because she would have spoiled everything, and I love him too much for that.

Lydia on the other hand is a different story. She didn't have to die, but I couldn't take any chances and she signed her own death warrant when I heard her continue to insist the wedding went ahead. I felt for sure, despite her selfish nature, she would be empathetic when Vivian died. Surely she would realise a death would have a profound, negative effect on festivities. I didn't imagine she would ever be happy with that – that's just not the Lydia I know. From listening to her argument with Aaron, it's like she wanted to get married at all costs, which makes me think there is something else going on. Something I'm not aware of. Still, that's of no consequence now.

My original intention with Lydia was just to make her ill enough, but with the option of finality if I should need it. I really hoped I wouldn't need it, I hoped she would see sense and we would get off the island without the wedding going ahead. The rest of it could be dealt with when we got back home. But no, she had to keep pushing and I just couldn't risk her talking Aaron into the wedding going ahead.

So, do you want to know how I did it? Of course you do, because although most of you could never do it yourselves, you're all obsessed with mystery and real life murder. Like people who slow down when they're going past an accident on the motorway to have a good gawp at someone else's misfortune. You secretly admire people who have the gall to do what you can't, or won't. You take a kind of perverse fascination in observing the mystery of murder unfold. Like watching a magician you are both desperate to know how it's done, but also realise once you find out, you can never not know.

Anyway, I digress. The simple answer is thallium salts, also known as the poisoner's poison. Thallium is the perfect toxin, it's a colourless, odourless and virtually tasteless heavy metal. Melissa and her research were absolutely on point. It used to be used in pesticides and rat poisons, but most countries have banned it now and it can be difficult to get a hold of. Unless you know where to look of course. (If you could see me now I'd be winking at you.)

A small dosage of salts dissolved in something like tea over a fairly regular period would definitely make someone unwell: muscle weakness, sore legs, Mees lines, alopecia and so on and so forth. Sometimes it can be mistaken for a B12 deficiency and sometimes the doctors just don't have a fucking clue – a bit like Lydia's doctor.

When I realised I was going to have to put an end to Lydia, I simply added a killer dose to her bottle of water. It was as easy as that. I even handed it to her.

Darius was even easier to get to. A bit of aconite in his hand gel and bob's your uncle. You might know aconite as Wolfsbane – that familiar weapon against werewolves! I know, I know, but it amuses me. Wolfsbane actually flowers all over the south west of England and is *so* easy to get a hold of it's ridiculous.

Remember: I did warn you about how simple it is to poison someone.

CHAPTER FORTY

REX

R ex knew the only way to be sure his son's name was cleared was to confess. He had hoped it wouldn't come to this, but he also knew that it might and had prepared for such an eventuality. If it had to come out he knew he didn't want Aaron to hear it third hand. He could just imagine how some Bajan policeman would portray the story to Aaron, without emotion or any sense of the reasons *why*. They would simply tell him his father had confessed and that would be an end to it.

That wasn't enough for Rex, he needed to be certain Aaron understood he had done it all for him. Rex needed to be satisfied he appreciated the life he was being offered, being assured, and that Aaron would go on and live it to its fullest.

Rex had been mulling over his options ever since Archibald had accused Aaron and set forth his evidence, weak as it was. Almost immediately he had realised he might need to own up and if that was the only course of action left open to him, he wanted to be sure he had it all straight in his head. Rex would need to give the letter to Aaron.

He had gone into detail when it came to each of the poisons he'd used, he wanted there to be no ambiguity. The police would almost certainly be shown the confession and he had to be positive there would be no suspicion that Aaron had forged it. Rex laid out his reasons why and signed off by apologising that Aaron had been a suspect and telling him he loved him – something Rex had not done often enough in the past.

Rex picked up his hip flask and swallowed down several mouthfuls of the whisky he'd bought in Duty Free. The sting and the warmth were familiar bedfellows. Whisky seemed to make everything so much easier to face, often it had been the only way he could face being married to Vivian. He caught Aaron staring at him and as he turned to look at him, Aaron was shaking his head. Rex knew his son was ashamed of him, but then Aaron had no idea what Rex had had to cope with since before his son was born.

Averting his eyes, Rex took one more mouthful – what did it matter now, he wouldn't be drinking whisky again any time soon, and this was good stuff. He held the amber liquid in his mouth and rolled it around his tongue. He wanted to memorise the taste of it, feel the warmth and fire spread down into his stomach. He pulled out the folded sheet of paper from underneath the newspaper he had been reading and held it tight in his fingers.

Aaron's whole world view of him, already tarnished, was going to change. It would get worse before it got better and Rex could only hope he would be forgiven one day. That one day Aaron would understand why he'd done what he'd done and perhaps even be grateful.

'What's that?'

Rex didn't take his eyes from the paper. 'It's a note.'

'A note? For who? What about?'

'It's for you.'

'Me? Why would you be writing me a note? I'm right here.'

Rex could see Melissa looking at him with interest, probably wondering what kind of family she'd got herself involved with. *Don't worry, lass, it'll just be the three of you before long.*

He made to hand the note across the aisle and then stopped himself.

'Do I get to read it now? Or...'

Rex thought for a moment and then nodded to himself, his head and shoulders moving. Yes, he was ready for this. 'Try to remember, I only ever want you to be happy and I love you.'

'Jesus, Dad, I love you too, but this isn't like you.'

Rex handed over the note. 'Please, read it.'

Aaron took the folded paper from his hands, his eyes never leaving Rex's. He could neither do nor say no more.

He waited patiently while Aaron read his words. He watched his son's face and tried to gauge his reactions, guess his emotions, but Aaron gave away nothing. His expression stony.

Melissa looked back and forth between them, clearly desperate to understand what was happening. Rex was pleased she didn't ask questions, Aaron's were going to be hard enough to answer without being made to answer those of a stranger.

Rex's heart raced and it was as if he could feel each pulse in his body without touching it. Adrenaline coursed through his veins as he waited for Aaron to finish reading. His mouth dried and he struggled to swallow. He reached for his heart medication and swallowed two pills along with another slug of whisky.

Sod it.

CHAPTER FORTY-ONE

MELISSA

One hour to landing

Eyes locked firmly on Aaron as he read his father's letter, nothing else existed in Melissa's universe for those few minutes. She couldn't even begin to guess what he had written and, as much as she wanted to, she couldn't bring herself to interrupt Aaron. All she could do was wait and, when he was ready, he'd either tell her what was in the note or let her read it herself. Melissa could only hope it would be soon, because if she had to wait until some indeterminable time in the future, she might just burst.

Finally, after hours had passed in her mind, Aaron stopped reading and looked up; first at her and then at his father.

Melissa couldn't stop herself. 'Are you okay? What does it say?'

Aaron brandished the note towards her. Whatever it was, he wasn't going to say it out loud.

'I'm truly sorry, son.'

'How could you?'

'I was doing it for you. I only wanted you to be happy. Happier than I was.'

Melissa zoned out and concentrated on the words in front of her. Her vision tunnelled and she felt her mouth drop open. Rex? Rex was responsible? Swallowing down the knot that had started to form at the base of her throat, Melissa read Rex's confession several times over. She had to be absolutely sure she was reading what she thought she was reading.

After the fifth time, she knew there was no mistake. Rex had murdered his wife, his daughter-in-law-to-be and his son's best friend, and he was saying it was all so Aaron and she could be together. He did it because he wanted Aaron to be happy. In his warped, freakish mind he believed the only way that could happen was to remove the obstacles – people! – who stood in the way of that.

Melissa couldn't speak. She didn't have the words and she wasn't sure she could voice them even if she did. Never had the term 'mixed emotions' been so on point. Melissa was horrified and disgusted at what Rex had done, but at the same time, she was going to get to spend the rest of her life with the man she loved.

But it all came at a cost she would never have agreed to pay. Now Theo would have no grandparents to speak of. Her own parents had died a few years earlier, her mother of cancer, followed a few months later by her father – apparently of a broken heart. Now Vivian was dead too and Rex would be in prison, likely for the rest of his life. Yes, she would have everything she ever wanted, but there was a sadness inside her too.

'Dad! Dad!'

Melissa flinched at the sound of Aaron shouting.

'What's going on?' Archibald demanded from across the plane.

Melissa heard the telltale signs and scrambled for a sick bag, before she could even put her fingers on it, Rex had thrown up. His face was turning red and Melissa could see beads of sweat across his forehead. When he grabbed his chest, Melissa's fears were confirmed – Rex was having a heart attack.

'Does he have a heart condition?' Melissa asked, but Aaron wasn't listening. 'Aaron! Does your dad have a heart problem?'

'Yes, he-um-he takes pills.' Aaron still couldn't take his eyes off his dad.

'Rex? Rex, have you taken your pills?'

His eyes were wide and he could only nod.

'Do you have a spray or any aspirin with you?'

Rex shook his head frantically, panic was setting in.

'Someone press the call button, see if anyone has any aspirin. Quickly!'

There was very little Melissa could do with no equipment and no drugs to help. Rex had already taken his medication and any more would cause more harm than good. All she could do was keep him relaxed and reassure him.

Rex began to slip into unconsciousness as Charley strode through the curtains.

'What–?'

'I think he's having a heart attack! Bring me the defibrillator!'

Charley's eyes bulged for a second before she ran the way she'd come.

'Help me get him on the floor. Aaron!' Melissa punched him in the arm to bring him back in the room.

He snapped to attention and between them they wrestled

Rex to the floor. Shaking, Melissa checked his pulse, but her hands would not be still. She clenched her fists and breathed deeply. This time when she touched her fingers to Rex's neck they were steady.

'Is he...?'

'Sh!'

Nothing.

Melissa knelt in one of the seat spaces and leaned on Rex's chest. She compressed his ribcage with straight arms and willed him to come back to life.

'Melissa?'

She looked at Aaron, but said nothing. Her expression would tell him all he needed to know – this was serious – and her words wouldn't help.

A moment later, Charley rushed back into first class carrying a square green box, which she thrust at Melissa.

'Turn it on. I need you to turn it on for me.' Melissa continued with the compressions while she watched Charley fumble with the box. 'Is it on?'

'Yes.'

'Okay, I need you to help me.' Melissa ripped open Rex's shirt before returning to pressing on his chest. 'The instructions are very clear, you just need to follow them. I'm going to keep doing CPR while you work around me. If you don't know, ask me.'

Charley nodded, staring at the box.

'Now! Let's go!'

Melissa watched as Charley peeled one of the pads from the backing plastic and placed it on the right side of Rex's chest, followed by the other pad on his lower left side. Wires trailed from the pads and attached to the defibrillator, which would hopefully save Rex's life.

Evaluating heart rhythm.

Aaron and Charley stared in surprise as the box spoke and then Melissa stopped compressions.

'Everybody stand clear, nobody touch him.'

The defibrillator gave the same warning before announcing it was about to deliver the shock. Rex's whole body jerked. Shock was the correct word.

Shock delivered. Provide chest compressions.

Melissa continued with CPR, waiting for the defibrillator to decide if it wanted to administer another shock.

Two minutes later, after re-evaluating the heart rhythm, it announced it was going to do just that. Melissa, Aaron and Charley could do nothing but watch and wait to see if this shock was any more effective than the last.

Shock delivered. Provide chest compressions.

Melissa jumped into action once more, but her hopes of saving Rex were dwindling. If the defibrillator couldn't save him, then nothing would while they were still in the air.

After another two shocks were delivered, Melissa calculated she had been administering CPR for at least fifteen minutes, meaning Rex had been experiencing a cardiac episode for almost twenty-five. How long should she keep going for? She looked at the faces around her, pleading through her eyes for them to help her make a decision. She wasn't a doctor; doctors decided when enough was enough, not nurses.

The looks of compassion from Charley and Daphne almost broke her. Aaron was still in shock and Archibald's expression was stony.

'I think he's gone,' Charley whispered.

Aaron looked at her with alarm, but Melissa was inclined to agree.

'No, please...' Aaron wasn't ready to give up yet.

Melissa thought about it for a moment and then said, 'We'll give it one more shock, just to be sure.'

No one breathed as they watched the defibrillator administer its final shock to Rex's prone body.

Shock delivered. Provide chest compressions.

'I'm so sorry.'

CHAPTER FORTY-TWO

AARON

The Runway, Grantley-Adams Airport, Barbados

A aron stared out of the window into the darkness. The aeroplane had landed around half an hour previously, but they had been ordered to stay on board and police officers would be with them shortly.

With the exception of Melissa and Theo, the rest of the passengers from economy class had been allowed to disembark after being informed the police would be in contact in the next few days to take their statements. Aaron wondered why they were bothering. No one had seen anything since it had all happened upstairs.

Aaron had lost both his parents in a matter of hours and the newsreel showing the events of their deaths was playing on a continuous loop in his mind. He knew neither of his parents had led a particularly healthy lifestyle, you only had to look at his mother's painkiller addiction and the fact his father carried a hip flask with him everywhere to know that, but he'd never thought they would be taken from him like this. He'd imagined long-term ill health and a chance to say goodbye properly.

After Melissa and Charley had made the difficult decision not to continue with CPR, everything seemed to happen first in slow motion and then at lightning speed. Charley had slowly packed away the defibrillator and Melissa had held him while he sobbed. His emotions were so confused: on the one hand he was angry with the man who had taken matters into his own hands and murdered three of the people closest to him. On the other, his dad had just died in front of him and no matter what he'd done, he was still his dad. And his dad loved him.

The next thing Aaron knew Charley was insisting they all sit down and fasten their seat belts. A sense of urgency in her actions he did not understand until she pointed out they were due to land any moment.

Unceremoniously, they picked Rex up and put him back in his seat, fumbling to fasten his seat belt so he wouldn't move when the plane landed. Melissa had to rush back to her seat to be with Theo. This was his first flight and she needed to be there for him in case he didn't like the landing. It wouldn't be fair to let Maggie deal with him by herself after everything she had done for them.

Now Aaron looked around the first class cabin and he could hardly believe that when the flight had taken off he had expected to get married in a few days. When they had boarded, there were seven – actually probably six – happy people looking forward to two weeks of beautiful sunshine. None of them could have foreseen what might happen. Except, Aaron realised, that wasn't quite true. One person *did* know what was going to happen.

Maybe it's all my fault. If Aaron had only had the courage to stand up to his mother, to disappoint Lydia, then none of this would have happened. Yes, there would have been fallout, arguments, recriminations, but everyone would still have been alive. The doctor would surely surmise his father's heart attack was brought on by the stress he'd endured while they were in the air.

Aaron knew he and Melissa needed to have a long serious conversation about where they went from here. His father had orchestrated all of this so they could be together and he wanted nothing more, but did Melissa want the same thing? Could she bear to be with him knowing people had died for their relationship? Did she want to be with the kind of man who couldn't stand up to his own mother? Who took the easy route to avoid confrontation?

Only time and lots of communication would tell. One thing he did know, was that no matter what happened now, he would be the best father he could be to Theo. He would shower him with love and affection, making sure he wanted for nothing.

A commotion behind Aaron announced the arrival of the Bajan authorities. He was just pleased he was in an English-speaking country and there would be no need to wait for translators. He twisted in his seat and saw the men talking to Charley in low voices whilst they took in the scene before them. He wished more than anything he and Melissa could face this together, but he knew that would never be allowed. He understood why they had to remain separated for a while longer.

A second man pulled out his mobile phone and called for forensics to come on board. Aaron knew they had been told by the pilot while they were still in the air that it was likely the casualties had been poisoned by a fellow passenger, so none of this was a surprise. Aaron hoped he'd be able to clear everything up very quickly with the letter he held in his possession from his father.

'Are you Mr Aaron Fortescue?' The second man was standing in front of him.

'Yes.'

'Would you please come with me? We have some questions.'

'Of course.'

At the police station, Aaron answered all of the questions posed by the detectives and showed them the letter from his father. They eyed it suspiciously before taking it and sealing it in a plastic evidence bag.

They informed him their investigations would take some time and that all of the bodies would need to undergo a post-mortem in order to confirm cause of death in each case. Aaron was also advised he would need to register the deaths of his mother and father. Archibald and Daphne were taking care of Lydia. All the time he was travelling alongside corpses, Aaron hadn't considered the admin and logistics that would be required at the other end.

'What about Darius? Who will tell his parents?'

'We are liaising with the US embassy here on the island. We didn't want the Johnsons to find out from the media, so we have had to move quickly.'

Aaron nodded slowly in understanding. How would he ever be able to face Darius's family again?

'Can I go now?'

'Yes, but please do not leave the island. We have the contact details of your hotel when we need to reach you.'

'Do you know how long this might take?'

The detective gave a shrug a Frenchman would be proud of, but declined to articulate an answer.

All Aaron cared about was being reunited with Melissa and Theo. With her by his side he could face anything. And he had lost time with his son to make up for.

CHAPTER FORTY-THREE

MELISSA

Sandals Hotel, Barbados

Melissa stood on the balcony wearing a sarong over her black bikini. She was looking out over the pool and the view stretched onto the white sandy beach and turquoise sea. Behind her, in the bedroom, Theo was taking a nap on the enormous super-king-size four-poster bed.

After they had disembarked from the plane two days earlier, Aaron had insisted they stay with him at his hotel. Archibald had blustered over the offer, since the hotel room they would be staying in should have been his daughter's honeymoon suite. Daphne, however, had been quite tired of the whole thing and pointed out to her husband that it hardly mattered now and unless someone made use of it, thousands of pounds would be wasted.

Aaron had been summoned to the police station to answer some more questions and Melissa was waiting for him to return. He had promised her and Theo a day out at the beach, and she was looking forward to some semblance of normality. This would be their first day as a proper family she supposed. Assuming, of course, the police really were satisfied that Rex was to blame and Aaron hadn't had anything to do with any of the murders.

Murders – God. How had it even come to this? Even when Ryan was at his worst, she had never contemplated killing him. Even though she hated him, she knew murder was a step too far. Yet Rex had killed out of love and to protect his son. Melissa had spent the last forty-eight hours mulling that one over and still couldn't wrap her head around it.

Her thoughts turned back to Ryan. Was it true? Had Rex really pushed Ryan in front of a train? She wasn't sure how she felt about it. Whenever she thought he might never be able to intimidate her again, tension left her shoulders and her breathing slowed. Even though Rex said he had killed him to clear a path for Aaron, she felt as though it had also been a little for her, and Theo.

Melissa stepped back inside to check on Theo. Passing through the separate sitting room, she poked her head into the bedroom, Theo was still sleeping. She sat on the sofa and looked around, still in awe of the opulence that surrounded her. Before he left, Aaron had explained she could have whatever she wanted from the in-room bar. If she couldn't find what she wanted, she was to order room service, or summon their butler.

Their butler! According to Aaron everything was the butler's job. He would unpack for them, carry their bags for them, make dinner reservations, sort out their laundry and he had a mobile phone so they could contact him at all times. It had blown Melissa's mind a little bit and she had quietly refused the gentleman's offer to unpack her bags. Not only did it feel like a stretch too far, but she also did not want him judging her for her

Primarni specials. She was certain he was used to hanging up Ralph Lauren and Gucci garments.

Melissa screwed her face up and remembered what Aaron had said in reply. This was her life now, assuming she intended to spend it with him. Having butlers and maids and their every whim catered to was the rule rather than the exception. She was yet to be convinced and wondered how, or if, that could all be true and Theo still grow up and not be spoiled.

She stood and opened the fridge set in the cupboard below the large flat-screen television and pulled out a can of juice. She checked the caddy for ice and was pleasantly surprised to see it full. *Maybe I could get used to this life after all.* She giggled, adding some of the ice to a glass.

'What are you giggling at?'

Melissa jumped, some of the sparkling drink spilling onto the tiled floor.

'Sorry, didn't mean to make you jump,' Aaron said, pulling her into him.

'It's okay. Hang on, I'll just clean this up.' Melissa pulled away from his embrace, but he held her tighter.

'You don't need to do that anymore.'

Melissa stopped and looked at him. 'I don't care how much money you have–'

'We have.'

'Whatever. I don't care how much money there is, or how much the fancy butler guy costs, I can, and *should*, clear up a mess I made. And let me tell you something else, we *will* be teaching Theo the same.'

Aaron was smirking at her. 'I do love it when you get all adamant like that.'

Melissa smacked his chest, but couldn't help smiling back at him.

'Anyway,' she said, crouching down with some tissue, 'what did the police say?'

Aaron's face turned serious. 'They said there's still a lot of investigating to do, but that we can go home. They can't rule me out completely right now, but by the looks of things, there's no reason to believe I was involved.'

'That's wonderful news!' Melissa embraced Aaron in a tight hug.

'Do you want to go home? I mean, I know we will have to eventually, but why don't we stay here and enjoy a holiday? I can get to know my son.' A gentle smile formed on Aaron's lips as he said the words.

'I'd love that,' she said and then kissed him passionately.

'Mama?'

Melissa and Aaron broke apart, laughing.

CHAPTER FORTY-FOUR

AARON

Six months later

'Cheers to us!'

There was still a part of Aaron that felt guilty about moving on with his life after the events on the aeroplane six months earlier, but he saw little other choice. Theo needed a happy and healthy mum and dad, so he could grow up in a loving family.

And Aaron had wanted them to be just that, a family. So once the funerals had taken place and the media furore had died down, Aaron had proposed to Melissa and she had said yes. Yes, but with the caveat that it just be the three of them. They had no family left anyway, but she had said she would feel 'a bit yucky' – her words – if they had any kind of celebration with their friends.

Today had been the day. Just before lunch they arrived at the registry office dressed up as if they were going out to dinner. Once there they asked two random strangers to be their witnesses and said their 'I do's with just seven people in the room.

Now they were in Aaron's favourite restaurant having lunch and their own little celebration.

'This is a bit fancy. What if Theo starts crying?' Melissa had whispered to him.

'It is fancy, but we're celebrating, even if it is just the three of us. I don't want everything we do to be marred. And if Theo starts crying we'll deal with it.'

Melissa didn't look so sure. 'I don't want to disturb anybody though.'

'You're worrying about things before they're a problem again,' Aaron said kindly. 'Please, try to relax and enjoy yourself. This is the first time I've managed to unwind since we got back from Barbados and I want you to have fun too.'

Melissa beamed at him. 'I'm sorry, you're right.' She squeezed his hand and looked at the menu.

It was true, Aaron really did feel like he could unwind and properly relax. The funerals were long behind them, but it was only a day or two earlier they'd received word the cases had all been officially closed.

Vivian, Lydia and Darius's post-mortems had all confirmed they had been poisoned, by various means. Rex's confession and the subsequent search of the house where police had found his chemistry paraphernalia confirmed he was the murderer. CCTV also showed him to be at the railway station where Ryan had met his demise.

Aaron had worried for a moment when his father's autopsy results had shown an excess of digitalis in his blood. Of course it was expected there would be some, it was in his heart medication after all, but it should not have been there in such high quantities. Traces of digitalis had also been found in Rex's hip flask, which pointed to an overdose. The police concluded he had suicided; death being preferable to a lifetime in prison.

Thankfully nobody had really thought to question why he wouldn't just swallow an excess of pills instead of dispersing them in his whisky, otherwise Aaron could have been in serious trouble.

He thought back to when he had first read his father's letter after he'd found it in his bag while looking for paracetamol. He had been so consumed with anger, he thought nothing of breaking ten tablets into Rex's whisky, knowing at some point, whether on the plane or after they landed, his father would drink the lot.

A taste of his own medicine, you might say.

THE END

ACKNOWLEDGEMENTS

To be perfectly honest with you, I never thought I'd have the opportunity to write one set of acknowledgements in a book I'd written, let alone a second set. Here goes!

First and foremost, I'd like to thank my publisher, Bloodhound Books. Betsy, Fred, Tara, Hannah and Abbie, you have always had my back and I know more than most the work that goes into getting a book out there. Thank you for all your hard work.

Thanks go to by editor, Morgen; my proofreader, Shirley; and my beta-reader Maria. You guys rock!

Betsy – as ever woman, you were a legend while I was writing this. It was hard and I made it hard work for myself, but you believed in me and my book, and helped me get across the line!

HUGE thanks have to go to all the readers, bloggers, book reviewers and anyone who shares bookish content. None of what us writers do would be possible if it weren't for you.

Every now and then, someone walks into your life and you just know they are for you. At the time of writing, technically I have only met Jen Faulkner, author of Keep Her Safe, five times, but that's just a number. This incredible woman has had my back for over a year now; she beta read The Flight and she's alpha reading book 3 for me as I type. Whenever we get together, time just flies by as we put the world to rights and talk about books, authors, publishers, agents and anything else that takes our fancy. Thank you, Jen.

I couldn't have written this book without the help of Charley Crocker. Charley answered a LOT of questions about aeroplanes, equipment, procedures, protocols and all manner of other things. I cannot thank you enough, if it weren't for you writing this book would have been a lot harder than it already was. And yes, Charley White the Cabin Crew Manager is named for Charley – it was the least I could do.

I must also thank Jay Emordi and Anita Skinner for helping me out with some medical questions during the editing process – you ladies were absolute lifesavers!

To my fellow Teletubbies, Patricia Dixon, Keri Beevis and Nathan Moss, thank you for all the love, support and motivation.

My non-bookish friends have never wavered in their support and enthusiasm from Open Your Eyes to this one. Joe, Di, Pete, Grace, Mike, Polly, El, Kezia, Beckie and Janice – thank you!

If you know me, then you know I love a book festival, and these guys help to make it them the incredible weekends they always are: Anne, Mik, the two Robs, Danny, Effie, Jen, Howard, Debbie, Norman, Lesley, Jack and Abir – thank you for your friendship! (If I've forgotten you – sorry, clearly I spent too much time at the bar with you!)

My family have been so incredibly supportive I can hardly believe it. Mum, Dad, Pamela, Craig, Lily, Teddy, Ivy and Henry, I love you all. Thank you for making all of *this* feel so special.

My final word has to go to my husband, Stuart. Stuart isn't really a reader, but that doesn't stop him supporting me in everything I do. He understands when I need to write, when I need to read and when I go off galivanting around the country without him. If it weren't for his love, support, motivation and inspiration I'm not sure any of this would be possible. And he's still better at telling people I'm an author than I am! Thank you for everything, honey.

A NOTE FROM THE PUBLISHER

Thank you for reading this book. If you enjoyed it please do consider leaving a review on Amazon to help others find it too.

We hate typos. All of our books have been rigorously edited and proofread, but sometimes mistakes do slip through. If you have spotted a typo, please do let us know and we can get it amended within hours.

info@bloodhoundbooks.com

Made in United States
Orlando, FL
07 March 2023

30793816R00150